THE NEW BIZARRO AUTHOR SERIES

PRESENTS

GUTMOUTH

GABINO IGLESIAS

Eraserhead Press

Portland, OR

THE NEW BIZARRO AUTHOR SERIES
An Imprint of Eraserhead Press

ERASERHEAD PRESS
205 NE BRYANT
PORTLAND, OR 97211

WWW.ERASERHEADPRESS.COM

ISBN: 1-62105-070-X

EDITOR'S NOTE

Gabino comes to novella writing as a fan and aficionado of horror and bizarro entertainment. When I asked if he'd considered writing a book, he sent me this dystopian tryst about a guy with a sentient mouth in his navel. And I loved it.

Gutmouth's world has been lovingly crafted in Gabino's bizarro-marinated brain—it's a living, breathing, horrid universe where technology, advertising, possibly aliens, and marketing are combined into a *1984, Naked Lunch, Idiocracy, Mad Max* sort of place where just staying alive for a day is a trick. With amputation and other mutilations as part of sexual satisfaction, simple mis-steps leading to torture, and quick-acting mutations resulting from the myriad products designed by the mysterious corporation that seems to be in charge of everything, this story is set in a place I'd never want to be. But reading about it is fantastic! This is a love story, an adventure, and a great bizarro representation of *The Odd Couple*. I'm happy to not have a snarky, mean mouth under my belly button. After you read this, I'm sure you will be, too.

I'm happy to present Gabino Iglesias' book as part of the New Bizarro Author Series. The NBAS strives to bring new voices in bizarro fiction to our readers. It serves as an opportunity to introduce you to new writers, and introduce them into the world of being an author. Eraserhead Press is happy to bring new, weird voices to you in the hopes that these authors will prove themselves to be strong members of the bizarro community and continue to entertain you for years to come. The publishing of this book marks the beginning of a one year proving period. Please help support our NBAS writers in their endeavors by telling your friends about their cool new books. The book you hold is only one of several hundred that must be sold in order for this author to continue on his path. We hope you help him along as best as you can. Thank you.

~~Kevin Shamel

AUTHOR'S NOTE

This book is dedicated to:

Ady for putting up with me.

Mis viejos por dejarme ser raro.

Carlton Mellick for offering encouraging words, pointing me in the right direction and being a friend as well as a source of inspiration.

Kick-ass author, friend and editor Kevin Shamel. Kevin's support, energy and guidance are the reasons this book is in your hands. No matter what goes down, you can count on Kevin to be fucking awesome. Thanks, Kevin!

I'd also like to thank Justin T. Coons for the great cover art, and all the authors that keep my brain in shape.

"Why would a woman, after going though the exhausting process of selecting and attracting a mate, securing his long-term love, and making vows of commitment, suddenly decide to risk it all for a fleeting moment of sexual pleasure – a transient delight than can put her life in peril? This question has baffled scientists for decades, but we now have a fundamental outline of the answer. Mating, like murder, has multiple motives."
- David M. Buss

"Quise mucho a esa chica, pero espero que no vuelva nunca más."
("I loved that girl a lot, but I hope she never comes back.")
- Quique González

"Perverseness is one of the primitive impulses of the human heart."
- Edgar Allan Poe

"The biggest example of ambivalence is that love and hate are possible toward the same individual. It is possible to have this dual set of feelings toward women."
- Dr. Edward J. Kelleher

ONE

A dripping noise jolted me awake. My pupils had adjusted to the darkness of my surroundings over the preceding days, and I was able to distinguish almost everything inside my tiny, sporadically-grumbling cell the moment my eyes opened.

The sound came from somewhere to my right. I scratched the sleep out of my eyes and used my nails to dig the crust out of my lacrimal sacs. The huge eyeball that scrutinized my every move was leaking a brownish liquid from a small crack underneath it, where it was tied into the soft, corrugated pink wall.

The thick substance dripped into a puddle on the floor. The drops sounded like a faraway slap on a fat ass. A furry, froglike creature lapped at the edge of the puddle with a hairy gray tongue. I tried hard to ignore the whole situation but soon the repetitive drip/slapping noise shredded my last nerve.

Anger boiling in my chest, I stood up and started punching the ocular nightmare on the wall. The first few punches did no damage but then I felt it cave a little. I kept at it until the crystalline membrane covering the eye shattered. The eyeball's inside was warm and spongy. I punched until the warmth was wrapped around my arm, all the way up to the elbow.

When I pulled my arm out it was covered with dark green sludge that smelled like putrid meat and burnt car oil. The froglike creature jumped up and squirmed its way inside the remaining pulp with a sound somewhere between a shriek and a whistle.

In the back of my mind I expected the walls to contract or shudder in reaction to the attack but they remained still—almost as if the eyeball had no direct connection to them.

The sound of jingling keys announced the arrival of the guard. I plopped my ass back on the bed and waited for whatever punishment was coming while trying to ignore the stench coming off my arm.

"Ssssstop it right now!" The guard hissed even before reaching the bars outside the cell.

"Eat shit and die," I told him.

A huge figure appeared, blocking the outside light. I could only make out a massive outline in the threshold—a blocky body with a pointy head. The thing standing outside the cell door breathed like a wounded beast and smelled like rotting fish and ammonia. A tentacled hand rested on his hip and snaked around as if independent from his body. I knew what was beneath the snaking digits and found myself craving a dose of the oblivion that gun could bring. For a man deprived of his freedom, a shock of electricity is nothing compared to the subsequent bliss of a few hours of unconsciousness.

"What did you do?" asked the figure.

"I poked Big Brother in the eye."

"You won't get any food today, assssssshole," the creature sibilated.

"Great," I said. "I don't want to eat your shitty slush anyway."

The brute slithered away, emitting a hiss that was his version of chuckling. I screamed after him, wanting to slip into a coma for a while. The guard ignored my cries and glided away until the hissing had faded out. The snot trail left in front of the cell door wafted in and smacked me in the face. I felt like crawling farther into the cell, but knew that the smell would still reach me there. I also knew it would linger for a few hours, hanging heavy in the air, choking me and pulling at my last strand of sanity.

"Nice going, featherbrains," Philippe blurted out.

I lifted my shirt and stared at the mouth under my navel. Hatred began to gnaw at me. I thought of punching the mouth, but previous experiences taught me it was useless.

"Shut up, you fucking aberration. You're the reason we're here in the first place," I said.

Philippe smiled a crooked grin in response.

"I'm hungry, mate. You think we can get some curry in here?" asked the toothy hole.

"I'm going to let you starve, you snaggletoothed prick," I said.

"For a bloke who couldn't satisfy his lady you sure sound like a macho man ready to take on all comers. You muppet," responded the mouth in his British accent.

"You know what? The best thing about dying is taking you with me," I told him, pulling my shirt down. The fact that Philippe remained quiet meant that, despite his bravado, he was finally feeling the pressure—fearing the audible steps of our impending doom.

TWO

The walls inside the cell resembled the lining of a stomach. Sometimes they would shudder powerfully. Their movement made me feel rejected and scared, like an unwelcome human ulcer or a piece of poisoned food. The fact that they quivered more than usual on that second morning had soured my mood. The repairman and his assistant were about to pay for it.

An argument between Philippe and I was in full swing. We disputed whether the reports of bull sharks with guns mounted on their heads showing up in Arkansas' portion of the Mississippi river were true or just another publicity stunt by the state's Department of Parks and Tourism to bring tourists there.

The guard's molluscoid form appeared outside the cell and cut the squabble short. "You have a vissssssitor, asssssssshole. You better behave yoursssssself."

"Go stick an electric eel up your ass, you octocunt," I replied.

The door swung open. A very short man wearing stained blue overalls and rubber boots stepped inside the cell just before the guard shut it and slithered away.

The standard-issue pot-belly and receding hairline made the man remarkably unremarkable. Only one thing stood out: silvery scales covered his balding pate—out of control psoriasis. The repairman carried a white bag and a red toolbox. He put them down without having to bend much, and I noticed something beside his leg.

A rat-like creature stood there, looking back at me and wearing a blue yarmulke. "What the fuck are you looking at?" asked the rat. "First time you see a Jewish ferret?"

Before I could reply, the man cut in, "We're here to fix the Watcher you broke." I caught a whiff of rotten eggs and camembert cheese. "Do your thing, hombre," I said.

"I would appreciate if you didn't break it again. Changing these things isn't easy."

"Yeah, you punk, mellow the fuck out," screeched the ferret.

"I won't make any promises," I told them with a wink.

The comment, or the wink, hit the repairman like a kick in the balls. The pudgy little fellow frowned. He bent over, flipped the toolbox lid open and pulled out a long screwdriver with a sharpened, shiny spoon at the tip. Shaking it menacingly in my direction, the man mumbled something. His voice climbed a few decibels before I could make out what he was saying.

"… you scumbags breaking everything! Yesterday some asshole decided to try to gnaw his way out of here. You know how long it took me to grow enough tissue to cover the hole? I had to patch it up and then stick around in case the biowall rejected it!" The man's gelatinous jowls shook as he spoke. The violent head movements triggered a release of silvery scales from his bald dome.

The ferret started screaming at the man, telling him to stick the screwdriver up my ass.

I stared at the snowing scales and tried to keep cool, but the stench coming from the repairman's mouth made it impossible. With one swift movement I jumped forward and snatched the screwdriver from his hand. The man and the ferret looked stunned.

The ferret reacted first. "Give it back right now, pus-face!"

The ferret's boldness pushed the repairman into action. "First you destroy the Watcher and now you take my tools from me? Do you know how much that tool costs? Is that why you're here? For taking stuff from hard-working people and honest rodents?" The repairman's bitter proletariat discourse made my blood boil. I grabbed the man by a few strands of greasy hair on his scaly dome.

"Hey! What do you…?"

A kick sent the ferret flying. I turned to dig out the repairman's left eyeball with the little spoon. It popped out easily. I held it as the repairman flopped to the floor in agony.

Screams echoed down the hallway. I could hear the ferret praying in Hebrew somewhere outside the cell. The thrashing man's leg bumped against the white bag and a new Watcher rolled out. I stomped it until only a viscous mess remained.

When the squid-guard showed up, I threw the repairman's eyeball at him. It flew through the bars, its stringy optic nerve flailing behind it like a sick comet, and hit the guard in the chest.

The guard's serpentine arm quick-drew his gun, and a heart-stopping, soul-crushing cramp took over me— knocking me down. The last thing I saw was the ferret standing in front of the guard, flipping me the bird with both paws.

THREE

Consciousness came via someone slapping me in the face with a dead squid. The unbearable smell and the sickly smacking snapped me awake.

I could barely open my eyes—they were stretched tight toward my ears. I felt a flat surface under me. I heard a gurgling noise: Philippe was either trying to speak or finally choking to death on some unsavory morsel.

The guard stood above me, slapping my face again and again. Instinctively, I tried to use my arm as a shield, but it wouldn't respond. The staccato hissing sound emanating from the guard's throat told me the son of a bitch was truly enjoying himself.

"That's enough," said a voice from behind the cephalopod tormentor. "Can't you see he's already awake?"

The guard stopped smacking me with the gooey tentacles. I unsuccessfully tried to get up again. My body felt like a gelatinous blob. What had been somewhat hard muscles now only managed to shake a bit when I tried to use them. A garbled squawk escaped my throat.

A few monstrous insects hung from a dark ceiling above me. The bugs seemed to be the only source of light. They looked like giant ticks. They dangled from the roof by unseen mouths, while their engorged bodies emitted a pulsating green glow.

"Relax, Mr. Dedmon," said the voice. "There's nothing to be afraid of."

The asshole guard stepped out of my way, and I saw a pasty, rail-thin man with no hair. His lab coat was so white it seemed to radiate white light.

"If thisssssss dicklesssssss bag of dogssssssssshit givesssssss

15

you any trouble, jusssssst call me," hissed the guard.

"We'll be okay, officer, thank you for your assistance," replied the skeletal man without looking at the guard. "Mr. Dedmon's behavior will be exemplary whether he wants to or not, isn't that right, Mr. Dedmon?"

Faced with the inevitability of my situation, I tried to agree via a silent nod, but nothing happened.

A lock clicked somewhere toward the back of the room and the skinny man bent down very close to my face. "Mr. Dedmon? I hope you're feeling a tad better. My name is Dr. Kahoohalphala and I'm here to study your brain."

I tried to speak. I wanted to ask the doctor what the hell was wrong with me, but my mouth barely budged and my tongue flopped out—drooling saliva. I felt the dribble slowly roll down my flattened features.

The man hovering above me looked like a lumpy version of the clichéd movie alien: tall, big head, huge eyes, long arms. His smile made the sides of his mouth creep up only slightly. "Do not try to speak, Mr. Dedmon," he said. "I will explain your situation to you to the best of my abilities, yes?"

Again I tried to nod with null results.

"I have administered an intravenous compound that made your bones soft and rubbery. You can rest assured the effects are not permanent. Consider it merely a temporary state of osteomalacia we were forced to give you in order to protect me from your explosive bouts of violence, yes?"

As the doctor spoke, I noticed his lack of facial hair. No eyebrows, no beard, no hair on top of his head and no eyelashes. A thin coat of a translucent substance covered the doctor's skin and made it shiny. It reminded me of a glazed donut.

"In order to protect the integrity of your skeletal system the compound currently coursing through your system contains a non-corrosive, non-acidic vinegarlike substance that ensures nothing will break," said the doctor. "I have also given you a strong muscle relaxant to further prevent you from any unnecessary outbursts."

Kahoohalphala sat down beside me and grabbed my deformed head with both hands. I felt it rise a few inches in his clammy hands. The doctor then brought his face six inches from my forehead and closed his eyes. Given the considerable girth of his head, I feared for a second the doctor would topple on top of my inert body.

"This procedure might strike you as bizarre, Mr. Dedmon, but I assure you it will be almost painless. You need to understand that simply asking you a series of questions would be an utterly useless exercise, yes? Your psychological inability to cope with your current situation coupled with the fact that you were a MegaCorp employee make you a valuable subject to our ongoing research. In other words, you wouldn't be subjected to any of this if we didn't think the data gathered from the study could help us with future patients, yes?"

While Kahoohalphala spoke, a bump began to develop on his wrinkle-free forehead. After a few seconds, a small white tendril burst out of the bump, almost like a huge blackhead that just got squeezed. The white coil jerkily wormed its way towards my forehead and pierced the skin above my right eyebrow.

I felt my head expand as my now soft cranium was pushed open by the intruding coil. A blink later I found myself standing on the street where I had once lived, right in front of the building that housed my apartment. The street was empty and the wind howled its way through some filthy nearby alley.

"This is only a recollection, Mr. Dedmon," said Dr. Kahoohalphala.

I turned to find the doctor standing about ten feet behind me.

"Attacking me here would be wholly ineffective and would only go a long way towards the acceleration of your pending punishment," said the doctor.

"Mellow out, doc, I wasn't planning on it," I replied, trying to ignore the fact that tearing out the doctor's jugular had crossed my mind.

"That's good to hear."

"Where are we? What the hell are we doing here?"

"This is a composite of your memories, Mr. Dedmon.

You are actually in control of what you think you're seeing. In this environment it will be easier for you to tell me what drove you to…dispose of your partner with such thuggish tactics."

"I see," I said while looking around.

A rat ran out of a hole somewhere to our left and scurried his way down the empty street.

"As you can see, Mr. Dedmon, you have a hard time letting go of the past. The presence of regular rodents tells me your recollections predate MegaCorp's governance."

"Guess so, doc. Maybe life was a tad better before you guys came along."

"Tell me about that life, Mr. Dedmon."

I approached the doctor and noticed he was at least eight feet tall. "Well," I said while taking a look around, "the city was a mess, but at least we had rats. Regular rats."

"Do you miss the rodents, Mr. Dedmon?"

"I don't know."

"What do you miss?"

I looked up at the dark sky. Huge artificial asses hung from extension poles on top of every lamppost. The asses had been installed as method of crowd control when the whole New World transition began. The devices were designed to rain down acid diarrhea. Kind of like a postmodern version of a lachrymatory agent with an olfactory punch. They had been one of the worst ideas MegaCorp had actually tried to implement.

"I don't miss anything," I said, my eyes still on the mechanical butts.

"Then why did you eliminate cyber-service provider #1,344,617?"

"Because that deceitful cunt betrayed me!" The scream, just like the rush of emotions I suddenly felt, came out of nowhere.

"So you believe the killing had nothing to do with the changes brought on by MegaCorp?"

"It had everything to with MegaCorp."

"How so, Mr. Dedmon?"

"Because this damned thing started it all," I replied while

lifting my shirt. Underneath it, my belly was whole again; no hole, no teeth, no Philippe.

"You blame your silly mutation for the crime?"

"You know what, doc? Fuck you."

"I see this crime is the result of a flawed coping mechanism. I don't think any of our products had anything to do with it," Kahoohalphala said looking skyward.

"Who the fuck are you talking…"

A sound resembling the mysterious "bloop" of a few decades prior, which eventually turned out to be a Cthulhu fart, brought Dr. Kahoohalphala and me back to the room we had been in before our little trip to brainland.

I opened my eyes. The pulsating ticks glowed on top of me and the doctor had disappeared. The lock clanged open and then the door was slammed. There was a merciless pounding in my temples. Just looking at the pulsating light-ticks hurt as much as a hammer to the head. I closed my eyes and listened to Philippe's wet moaning for a while. At some point I drifted into sleep.

When I awoke, I was back in the pink cell.

FOUR

Accepting imprisonment was tough for me. My cell resembled an irritable stomach. The thrice-daily slush they served was actually edible, so my problem was not with the physical circumstances I had to deal with, although I was sure that could change at any moment. No, my despair came from being treated as a delinquent. Such treatment can be hard to swallow for those that consider themselves good people.

Although I had enough brain power to know that "good" was nothing but a floating signifier, my feelings were stronger than semiotics and those dictated that I didn't deserve to be locked up. I had never molested kids, cheated MegaCorp or kicked puppies around. In fact, I had even refused to buy one of those dogs with no legs that a small MegaCorp affiliate flaunted as the latest advance in pet convenience.

No more running after Spot!
Stop worrying about speeding cars!
These dogs will never go where they're not wanted!
No more jumping on the human-skin sofa!

The whole spiel had struck me as a fad, and I had reason to think so. Marie, my girlfriend, had bought into the previous pet craze: bottled cats. A small neighborhood MegaCorp pet store had managed to stick felines into bottles, but they had forgotten to leave enough room for them to take more than ten or twelve dumps. When the crap started to pile up, Marie had smashed the bottle. The result was a fat, wriggling, hairless, crimson worm with the head of a cat. One night, tired of listening to the unremitting gurgling meows, I flushed the damn thing away. Pets? No, thank you: I know how stupid animal-fashion can be.

20

Despite having flushed the Kitty-In-A-Kan, I did not consider myself an evil man. I had fucking feelings. In fact, I found myself craving some company. The brain-rape Dr. Kahoohalphala had performed on me had some side effects—one of them being the recognition that my predicament was the result of life playing a little trick on me.

Life, Philippe and Marie that is.

How I hated that two-timing one-legged whore! How I craved to strangle the petulant, back-stabbing British bastard under my navel! How my past life now seemed positively amazing!

I had been a repo man before MegaCorp took over. When they did, my tracking and recovering skills landed me a position as a hunter for MegaCorp. The job, as the name implies, involved hunting down people who refused to comply with MegaCorp rules and regulations and bringing them to the local Consumer Rehabilitation and Punishment Center. I would usually get a call or text with a crime, a name and an address and then I would track down dissidents—folks that refused to buy their allotted quantities of products each month, stubborn citizens who wanted to grow their own food, horny individuals that raped someone else's pleasurebots, things like that. From the inside of a cell, that life looked like paradise.

Catching criminals had been my life for about a decade and all those good memories were flooding my brain while I helped Philippe swallow the cerulean porridge.

While the mouth ate, I wondered about the tickling sensation in my lower abdomen. It had been there since my second day in prison and I was sure it forewarned some occurrence of epically shitty proportions.

As an insider of sorts, I knew that MegaCorp enjoyed using death row inmates as guinea pigs for new products. The magenta walls that surrounded me were probably radiating some brain-melting waves at me while the mouth chewed. Maybe the stuff Philippe was wolfing down so eagerly actually contained some new conscience-altering drug that would have me swallowing and then birthing myself through my ass just like that time Marie had talked me into trying her favorite drug.

Between the chewing and the fear, I was having a hard time not freaking out. The fact that Marie haunted me didn't help, either. Every time I thought about her, my sanity danced a tango at the edge of a gigantic black hole.

Torn between the way I loathed her and the love I had once felt, I couldn't help but feel like she had me in her claws and was slowly squeezing the life out of me. Marie's three marvelous breasts, brown tresses and soft stump bubbled from the dark recesses of my brain and kicked around the pieces of my broken heart. I also felt like sticking a sawed-off shotgun into Philippe and pulling the trigger.

"Can you swallow faster? I'm tired of feeding you." I started a conversation to keep my sanity.

"Pardon me for not having any bloody arms, Princess," replied Philippe, spewing purple crap all over the front of my legs.

The conversation didn't help much because it was always the same. We had started having it the second Philippe began asking for food. It made me dream about better days; days when I had only one mouth.

I had once been a normal guy, but after MegaCorp took over, everyone and their goddamned freckled, unicorn-dog developed some sort of mutation. Mine happened to be a mouth that grew just below my belly button. Well, not just a mouth—a fucking British prick of a mouth that wouldn't shut the hell up and was always hungry. Sadly, the mouth had also fucked Marie as a way of thanking me for feeding him every pathetic day of his limbless, dickless, aimless life.

Philippe had started like a big pimple I found one day while showering; a small, itchy, red bump that hadn't been there before. A few days later it turned into a nasty, purulent infection. I went out and bought a new psychotropic antibiotic that was supposed to use my own brainpower to heal the infection. After a few days taking it I went deaf and could only hear Stravinsky playing inside my head. It almost drove me to suicide. I stopped taking it the same day yellow-brown shit started leaking out of the hole.

I stuffed the hole with gauze and covered it with duct

tape, but it became bigger and then stopped hurting and oozing stinky stuff. The fact that the entire area went numb was as much of a relief as it was a worry. Procrastinating and not making an appointment with a Health Provider was about to turn into a life-changing experience.

When the whole mess started caving in, I decided to sit and wait for whatever was coming. Although I was afraid of the hole expanding and somehow killing me, sucking my body into a parallel universe inside my own stomach, it seemed improbable. The hole stayed the same size, but teeth came out and lips began to form. Before I had time to figure out what the hell was happening, a 9-inch tongue came out to explore as I watched a chapter from an interactive book. A month later, the hole started talking.

Food. It would just ask for food. Constantly. After the thing ate, I felt full, so I guessed there was some connection between it and my stomach. Soon the conversations became a bit more elaborate. The mouth introduced himself as Philippe and waxed poetically on the perfect level of crunchiness olives should have, the ideal snap of deep-fried sausages, the unpleasantness of a carrot's texture and how Angora cats tasted better with a side of fried butter.

Unfortunately, the conversations didn't last long; our chemistry sucked and we couldn't stand each other. Philippe was misogynistic and racist, which made me feel guilty about having him. Plus, his extravagant tastes clashed with my financial reality. A hunter couldn't afford a steady diet of bipolar midget brains, Angora cats and chocolate-stuffed Greek olives.

The whole thing was bound for disaster, and after a rough night of drinking, disaster ensued.

I had been out with my friend Tony, indiscriminately imbibing PCP-laced absinthe and endorphin beers until reality became a bag of colorful worms singing opera.

After the drinking was over and the worms had quieted down a bit, I stumbled home and tried to get Philippe to wrap his wet, strong muscular hydrostat around my raging erection. The mouth refused and after I repeatedly tried to force-feed him, the fucker bit down on the head of my penis. Hard. The gushing blood freaked out both of us. The relationship was never again as cordial as it had been up to that point. In fact, I would eventually come to blame that night for the way Philippe had betrayed me later on.

Standing in a pink cell feeding Philippe, watching his long tongue come out to clean my surrounding pubic hair, I realized that procrastination was what had landed my ass in prison. If I had taken care of the pimple when it first sprouted, maybe my life would have continued its course with nothing of this crappy magnitude ever happening.

"All done, mate," said Philippe.

"You know we won't get anything else until dinner, so don't even think about asking."

"I thought you said you were going to let me starve."

"I forgot."

"You scatterbrained cunt."

"I'm really getting tired of your shit, Philippe."

"And just what are you going to do about it, mate?"

"I'll find a way to watch you die before I leave this world."

"Still bitter, are we?"

"Shut the hell up."

"If it makes you feel any better, I'm part of you, mate," replied the mouth with a giggle.

I wondered for the millionth time what would happen if I took a knife to my own gut.

FIVE

I woke up with a bloated stomach and something stirring in my bowels. Philippe remained strangely quiet, which meant he was also feeling something. Letting Philippe enjoy the purple porridge the guard brought us three times a day began to seem like a mistake.

I tried to take a crap twice, but failed to produce anything. Then, just as I was about to call the guard, something started coming out of me. I ripped my pants off and found the thing squirming around in my underwear just as a second one plopped out.

It took only one look for me to identify the cylindrical, fist-sized creature born from the depths of my colon. It was an overgrown acidophilus bacterium. It twitched around a little and I felt something that closely resembled affection.

More bacteria were slowly sashaying out of my ass so I spread-eagled on the bed and waited for the exodus. Afterward, I picked up all the seven wriggling giant bacteria, and gently placed them in the toilet. Flushing would mean the end of my new pets, so I started thinking about a solution to my new scatological conundrum.

Beside birthing some overgrown acidophilus, the day was dragging along like the rest of them. In a nutshell, I sat in bed trying to predict when the walls would shake next and hated Philippe with all my being.

Although concentrating on hatred struck me as a very unproductive enterprise, I couldn't help it. The teeth-hole had screwed my girl. True, Marie had allowed it to happen, but that bitch had already gotten what she deserved.

Marie had never been the perfect girlfriend. She was a one-legged stripper and cyber-prostitute who worked at a MegaCorp place called the Ampu-titties Club. I went there once to get some cyber-action and that's how we met. I came in, paid for half an hour, took a pill, strapped on a helmet, stuck my unit in a silicon tube, threw myself on the Spanish leather reclining chair and waited for the hum.

I had emailed them a fantasy the day before. Their recreation of my description was amazing.

After the hum, a perfect world came into focus. A brown linoleum floor stretched before me. Bonsai palm trees dotted the landscape and dead, skinned cats and marble Ed Gein busts hung from a turquoise sky by ropes made from the blondest, shiniest hair ever. In the distance, a group of shrieking furries ran for their lives as a giant basilisk chased them on two legs, alternatively shouting passages from the Bible and shooting the furries with an enormous shotgun cock.

As soon as the first furry went down in a gorgeous explosion of fake fur and real blood, I looked around for my hired companion, my mercenary of love. She stood right behind me—undoubtedly soaking in the otherworldly beauty of the place. Her perfectly round body and shiny, bumpy green skin were just what I had asked for. I grabbed her hand and together we ran toward the trail of dead and twitching furry bodies.

The linoleum was perfect for the slick sensation I wanted to achieve. I took the sweet avocado woman and gently laid her on the linoleum, right on top of a deliciously slippery mixture of furry blood and organ tissue.

We made hurried, passionate love under a swinging Ed Gein bust while screams, strange biblical names and shotgun blasts resounded in the distance. Just as I was about to pop, the avocado woman ripped open her own chest and pulled out a big seed. It was covered in green veins and pulsated in her hands. The woman cracked it open as I came and the light of the sun burst from it, blinding both of us just as the buzzer announced the sad end of the perfect fantasy.

This was not the first time I had created a great fantasy, but none of my previous lovers-for-hire had been as fervent and involved as this sweet avocado woman. On my way out, I slipped the equipment guy a few bills and got the name of the seductress: Marie.

I left the room with her name flashing in my head like a neon sign on steroids. I had to find Marie. I asked around and a fat man with no arms salivating at the edge of a stage told me her performance was about to start. I ordered a drink and lit a downer-cigarette to calm my nerves. A floating chair in front of the stage was empty, so I sat on it and waited.

The lights dimmed and the sound of revving industrial machinery came from the overhead speakers. On stage, a stump appeared. The round, scarred appendage teasingly bobbed up and down while the rest of its owner remained hidden behind the mauve velvet curtain.

When Marie finally came out the crowd went into a frenzy. I didn't blame them. She wore a bologna bikini and a Viking hat. The thin slices of fake meat barely covered the nipples on each of her three breasts. Her skin glistened like a wet olive. Hooting and hollering were accompanied by chest pounding and hair pulling. A gang of crazed baboons would've acted more civilized than the bunch of animals surrounding the stage.

A guy sitting two chairs away from me passed out and the kleptomaniac cockroaches that infested the city swarmed him, leaving the guy completely naked in a few seconds.

I stared at the marvelous dancer on stage. After some more posing and dancing, six scantily-clad, heavily muscled shemales brought out a huge fat woman on a stretcher and put her on the floor. An ear-splitting crescendo brought the sound of the machines to a sonorous climax as the shemales lubed up Marie's stump with some transparent substance that reflected the stage-lights.

When their job was done, the shemales left Marie alone. She began to move her hips back and forth, stabbing the air with her lubed stump. She approached the fat woman on the floor. The lard monster stuck her tongue out and opened her legs, exposing a dark, gaping, glistening hole that glistened. Marie slowly inserted her stump into the woman. The moans that escaped the obese lady's throat were like mating calls from a moose. Marie responded to the groaning and moaning by thrusting her stump deeper and faster in the wet cavern.

By the time Marie was done jumping with her slimy

stump buried deep inside the convulsing fat monster on the stretcher, I knew I had found the love of my life.

Ampu-titties soon became my nightly haunt. I went there for three consecutive weeks. Marie agreed to meet me outside of her work because she loved guacamole and assumed someone with such a tremendous avocado fetish couldn't be a bad guy.

For our first date, I took her to dinner at a taco stand. A seven-foot-tall blonde Amazon with piercing blue eyes and a Mexican accent served us a plate of fetus tacos, which, according to her, were made with the softest meat available. She said she had all the equipment, and grew the fetuses herself. Marie was a tad skeptical but after a few minutes she wolfed down half the plate along with a whole bottle of hot sauce.

With full bellies and jolly hearts we went back to my place to make sweet, sweet love. Afterward, staring out of my second-floor window and listening to the agonizing screams that came from the Genital Mutilation and Erotic Maiming Center downstairs, Marie told me how she had lost her left leg in an accident involving an experimental depilation cream a friend had talked her into trying.

I explained that with a salamander DNA procedure she could grow it back. She laughed at my naïveté and said her stump was a goldmine. I nodded like a bobble head doll and stared at the moonlight reflecting off the perfect curves of Marie's amazingly smooth and round trio of natural breasts. Looking at her, I realized how some mutations, when placed properly, can be a wonderful thing.

SIX

Marie was very clear with me from the start that she would not stop dancing or encountering men in cyberspace. Blinded by love, I agreed. Her job was not something to be worried about. But a few weeks after we started seeing each other on a regular basis I realized it had truly messed her up.

One night she pulled out a thin dildo covered in Brillo and asked me to use it on her. When I refused, she told me to get on my back. That's when one of our pre-sex staples began. She rubbed herself against the coarse hair on my belly. She rubbed herself hard. After that got started, she couldn't get going without the chafing action.

Right about that time I developed a painful pimple. At the beginning, the thought crossed my mind that it could be the result of all that hardcore rubbing. Maybe Marie had caught a virus on one of her cyber-romps. When the thing caved in and sprouted teeth, Marie decided I should keep my shirt on while we made love. Feeling self-conscious as hell, I agreed. She used my leg instead.

When Philippe started talking, he sometimes interrupted our conversations. Marie always found his disruptions witty and cute. If she was around and Philippe bitched about being hungry, Marie would whip something up or at least get him something from the fridge. The few times I jokingly mentioned something about it, she defended her actions by saying that Philippe did the chewing but the food was really for me. Without skipping a beat, Philippe would always chime in his agreement. My stump-obsessed, trio-of-breasts-addicted brain let me believe it was all about me.

Over time, all of my neighbors met Marie. She learned to keep her stuff tied down or locked up so that the klepto roaches couldn't get to it and our life as a couple fell into a blissful normalcy that I truly welcomed. Regardless of how full of psychopathic pleasurebot rapists, underground organic food growers and disgruntled buyers my day happened to be, going home to a glorious, three-breasted nymph that would kiss me tenderly and beg me to lick guacamole off her stump was more than enough to keep me going.

At work, my friend Tony kept making fun of my new-found good fortune. Tony worked at the Rehabilitation Center where I took the folks that had broken the law. Standing 6'4 and tipping the scales at 295 pounds, Big Tony was a bodybuilding enthusiast whose dreams of going pro had been killed by the same procedure he thought would take him to the top.

Tony once read in a bodybuilding magazine that pros were undergoing treatments with naked mole rat DNA. The creature's efficiency at oxygen intake, ability to alter its metabolic rate, resistance to cancer, lack of body hair and capacity for pain endurance made them the perfect mammal to mix with a steroid freak. Unfortunately, since Tony couldn't afford to get the Heterocephalus glaber injections from a MegaCorp treatment center, he wound up injecting some shit he got through the Internet that turned out to be common rat DNA. The end result was a coat of grey hair he couldn't get rid of, constant hunger, pointy ears and big front teeth at the end of a mouth that protruded a few inches from his face.

At the Rehabilitation Center, Tony was in charge of administering punishment to incoming subjects. Since I generally had nothing better to do between texts and thoroughly enjoyed the big rat's company, I usually hung around and helped him dish out whatever chastisement the regulations said applied to a particular criminal act. I did it so often that I had memorized some of the most common crimes and their penalties.

Not buying anything for more than a month got a person tied up and their head put inside a box full of hungry badger mice.

Selling anything and refusing to give MegaCorp their

half would get someone a two-inch steel pipe shoved up their ass followed by a cup of molten lead.

Raping or stealing another citizen's registered pleasurebot begot castration by a fat one-eyed dominatrix called Bella whose methods changed depending on her mood.

Trying to escape from a licensed MegaCorp agent, such as me, would cost you a foot. We would get it by placing the conscious prisoner's foot inside a Plexiglas cube filled with saw-toothed maggots. The grubs would eat the foot through to the bone, which we'd clip with bolt cutters afterward.

Regardless of the task at hand, Tony usually found time to make fun of me. According to the rodent man, trusting a woman was as brilliant as sipping on a mercury and cyanide shake. In his misogynistic opinion, women were as dangerous as a hungry, rabid dog, as trustworthy as a pedophilic snake and as useful as a handful of mucus.

Tony's comments would usually send Philippe into a fit of laughter that could last up to an hour. At the time, I took it all as friendly jabbing and smiled at his comments or told him he needed to get laid more often. Nevertheless, sometimes the Tony's words would float back to me when Marie was feeding Philippe or when she asked him if he was hungry while I was trying to talk to her about something else.

Then, on a day that had started like any other, Tony's ideas about even my woman being an evil, shiftless monster came to be illustrated.

Ever since Philippe had made its toothy, hellish way into our lives, Marie and I had made certain arrangements to keep the awkwardness out of the bedroom as much as possible. Besides me keeping my shirt on, we had politely asked Philippe to remain silent. As an extra measure, I sometimes covered him with duct tape, but Marie put an end to that immediately after she found out. Also, Marie's rubbing was done mostly on my thighs rather than my gut for fear of bumping into Philippe. Unfortunately, one drunken night all precautions were thrown to the wind and everything went to hell.

We had gone to see a performance by Motora, one of

Marie's friends from Ampu-titties. Motora climbed on stage and chopped off parts of her anatomy while reciting a powerful and poetic monologue about the impossibility of eternal love. She would name an unfaithful lover and then chop off her pinky finger with a butcher's knife. She'd then explain how testicle size directly correlates to the capacity for faithfulness and slice off one of her white breasts. After cursing the absence of a father figure in her life and blaming that deficiency for fucking up all her relationships, she chainsawed off her foot.

The performance was noteworthy and messy. Her message got across: love is incoherent, whimsical and dangerously erratic. For her big finale, she blamed her own selfishness for her inability to love and, after a whimpering elucidation of how love is nothing more than a series of chemical reactions, she stabbed herself in the chest with a sword. Blood spurted out of her mouth as she screamed the word love over and over again, crumpling to her knees. The crowd went nuts and everyone walked home with nice things to say about the performance and a bit of blood on their clothes.

Upon reaching the apartment, we decided to have a few drinks and watch the madness on in the street below. After knocking back a few and watching a guy beat a smaller man to death by grabbing him by the ankles and smashing him repeatedly against the wall, Marie decided to take off her prosthetic leg. The sight of her naked, sweaty stump turned me into a wild man.

I jumped on her, kissed her neck and carried her to bed. My tongue ran over every single pressure ridge the fake leg had left on her stump. Heavy petting followed and soon Marie was choking me with her panties while rubbing herself with the hairs on my belly. The rubbing grew wilder than ever and she twisted her lacy red panties around my throat tighter than usual.

Drunk and happy, I remained oblivious to what was going on until Marie began screaming passionately, her stump thumping against the side of my torso as if she was the victim of an epileptic fit. I stared at her in bewilderment as she clenched her eyes, bit her lower lip until blood ran down her chin and came in a trembling frenzy.

Marie collapsed on my chest gasping for air and then bounced back up with a distorted face that spoke volumes. I could see fear, anger and disgust jockeying for position on her delicate features.

With a swift move, Marie climbed off of me as if suddenly realizing I had the plague. As she separated her body from mine, Philippe's heavy, wet tongue slipped out of her and fell on my belly with a loud thud comparable to that of a dead octopus falling from a second story window. The slimy appendage immediately retreated into the hole it had come from.

Silence invaded the room. I felt frozen. I wanted to make sure what I thought had gone down had actually gone down. I turned to Marie. She was standing by the bed holding her hands to her mouth.

"Baby, what the hell just happened?" I asked, feeling like I was drowning.

"I don't know," she replied with a trembling, broken voice.

"What the fuck do you mean you don't know? Did Philippe do something to you?" My voice was rising but there was nothing I could do about it. Anger was blurring my vision and my heart climbed up to my throat where it proceeded to break all known speed records.

"I think...I think Philippe was inside me."

"Inside you? What...? Why didn't you stop him?"

I felt infuriated, betrayed, violated and abandoned. Gulping air in fast, short inhalations that were making me dizzy as fuck, I saw Tony's head hovering above the bed as warnings cascaded from his open mouth like mud sliding down a steep hill.

A scream from the street entered the apartment and broke the spell.

I got up, looked down at Philippe and took a swing. The uncomfortable angle prevented me from putting a lot of power behind the punch but it was enough to send me back a few steps. I felt no pain and Philippe didn't complain. I took another swing. Harder this time. It made contact with the yellow, crooked teeth. My knuckles were sliced open and blood began to pour out of Philippe's diseased gums.

"You know this is useless, you bloody wanker!" screamed the mouth.

"I'm going to kill you, you ungrateful, backstabbing son of a bitch!"

"Stop it!" yelled Marie.

Surprised by her guttural scream, I was thrown into inaction and silence.

"We need to calm the fuck down and figure out what just happened here," said Marie as she balanced on her one leg.

"I know what happened here. This arrogant fucker put his fucking tongue inside you!"

"Honey, I don't know..." Something in her voice triggered a thought: she had let him do it.

"Shut the hell up, you gimpy slut! Get the hell out of my house this very minute," the spit that came flying out of my mouth felt like acid. I could taste blood.

Marie looked surprised and hurt, as if my eruption was the least probable consequence of the preceding events. She stood there, balancing on one leg and looking at me with eyes filled to the brim with unshed tears. "Is that what you really want?" she asked in a resigned voice that almost made me feel guilty.

I thought for a second before replying. "I need to think about what just happened. I need some time alone."

"What you need to do is get her bum back in bed, you pillock," piped Philippe.

"Shut the fuck up right now, Philippe! Marie, leave. Please. Now."

Marie nodded slowly and hopped over to where her prosthetic leg was propped against the wall. The sight of her voluptuous ass bouncing around and the stump doing its little circular motion with every jump was the sexiest thing I had ever seen. The sound of breaking glass told me my heart had just shattered.

Marie threw on her dress, picked up her things, slapped the prosthetic leg on and left the apartment without a word.

I sat on the bed and listened to the rhythmic tick-tock of her high heels as she descended the stairs and exited the building. I kept listening as the sound grew dimmer and finally disappeared somewhere in the night.

I fetched a drink and pulled my buzzing head out of Marie's underwear. The panties flew and landed on a corner. It took less than a minute for the kleptomaniac roaches to make them disappear through a hole in the wall.

The rest of the night was a long, dark fog punctuated by painful shrieks that came from varying distances and climbed up to the window to remind me that the damned world was still out there, that monsters were feeding and that everything around me was as real and the pain in my chest.

Sleep finally took me just as day began to break and a gigantic winged platypus flew over the city in search of breakfast.

SEVEN

The morning after the debacle, I was awakened by screams coming from the Genital Mutilation and Erotic Maiming Center downstairs. By the sound of it, Screw, the owner of the place, was apparently sawing somebody in half with a rusty handsaw.

I envied the pleasure and pain that guy or girl was receiving. Walking to the window, I noticed the splattered blood and brain matter left behind on the wall from the guy used as a baseball bat the night before.. The gore on the wall was his only legacy. I wondered what mine would be, but the thought dissipated quickly.

It was Saturday and the prospect of spending two days holed up in a small apartment listening to Philippe ask for grub and dealing with the klepto roaches was not something I could manage without eating a bullet or trying to get rid of the mouth in my stomach with a steak knife. Knowing that eating a bullet would probably hurt, I decided to seriously contemplate the second option.

Very near to where Philippe began, my nervous system stopped being mine and belonged to the mouth. I couldn't feel him chew, talk, move or swallow. If I managed to cut around it while remaining inside Philippe's pain zone and out of mine, there was a slight chance of cutting him out in a few minutes.

With a scary resolution burning behind my eyes, I got up and grabbed one of the knifes I had under lock and key in the kitchen (I didn't want to find out what the crazy-ass klepto cockroaches could do if they got hold of weapons).

Using the sharp tip of the knife, I gently poked at my gut right below the belly button. Pain shot up all the way to my brain. Half an inch lower, the blade pressed into flesh but my brain received no pain signals. I pushed in a little deeper and the skin gave in, bouncing out a little and engulfing a quarter of an inch of blade.

"Hey!" screamed Philippe. "What the hell do you think you're doing?"

"Ah, so you felt that. Good. I'm getting rid of you once and for all."

"Are you off your fucking trolley, mate? You can't do that!"

"We're going to find out if that's true in a few minutes. Would you mind keeping your bitching to a minimum while I do this, please?"

"Listen, mate, getting rid of me would be bloody suicide."

"Sure," I said as I began a slow sawing motion that dug the blade in a little deeper.

"Hey! I'm fucking serious, you crazy cunt. I'm connected to your stomach!"

Philippe's words rang true. I would feel full after he ate. The slimy bastard was right. I pulled the knife out. Blood leaked, slow and warm. It was time to rethink the plan.

In order to get completely rid of him, I would have to dig to my stomach and sever whatever connection Philippe had to it. How deep I could cut without feeling pain was anybody's guess, and even with drugs to numb the pain, there would still be bleeding to deal with. Suddenly, getting rid of Philippe sounded like major surgery. Precisely the kind of shit you just don't do at home.

"Alright, you win," I said in a defeated voice.

"I never thought you'd get this bloody crazy, mate. Is this over that trollop?"

"Yeah, man, you stepped over the line with that one."

"That slopper had her minge over me for a few minutes, mate, what the hell did you expect me to do?"

"How about put up with it and keep your ugly snake-tongue to your own damn self?"

"Come on, mate, that's water under the bridge! Can't we just forget the whole thing ever happened and get ourselves some fry-up?"

"No, Philippe, we can't. What happened happened and the next time I see her, awkwardness is going to drown any attempt we make at having a normal conversation."

"Then don't see her ever again! I'll tell you this, mate, and don't get all pissed again, that bird wanted me ever since she first set eyes on me. She's no good for you. I think you're going to be better off without her."

"No," I replied. "It's not that easy. She broke something. She shattered what we had for nothing. She played with me. That's why she didn't quit her job after we started seeing each other, because she liked what she was doing with all those random guys in cyberspace, she got a kick out of making all of them go apeshit with her show, too."

"Then get rid of her."

"What are you talking about?"

"Bump her off!"

"I couldn't, she's…"

"She's a two-timing, one-legged moose, mate. In fact, if you don't kill her, she's bound to come crawling back into your life. Before you know it, she'll be grinding on my lips again and making you bloody miserable. Next thing you know, that cunt will be gangbanging the klepto roaches!"

"You really think she had a thing for you, don't you?"

"Are you mental? She found me funny, cooked me food, allowed me to insert my tongue in her gash and rode me until she almost passed out. Were you not there for all this, mate?"

"I guess I was. I…I need some time to digest all this. Just leave me alone for a while, will you?"

"No problem, but keep in mind what I told you."

The conversation left my head spinning so I decided to go out for a mind-clearing walk.

Without having breakfast, I got my clothes and shoes from the safe, dressed and left. My feet carried me straight south to Shlicker Park. I sat on a bench, eyes still blurry with drink, heart broken and senses reeling. For the next few hours, I sat and watched the serpent-trees snag bloated pigeons in mid-air. The crunching of their tiny bones mixed with the frantic cooing from the survivors to create a perfect melody for a Saturday morning in the park.

Street performers were power-vomiting into plastic baskets set about fifteen feet from them. A parade of sad individuals walked through the park, lovingly dragging a plethora of indescribable monstrosities from all sorts of leashes. Old geezers met in a corner to play a bit of explosive chess, but the whole thing ended up in a half-assed geriatric fistfight. A naked midget with a tattooed-on kimono appeared out of nowhere and began giving a martial arts demonstration with nunchucks made of toothy, hairy teratomas.

Through all this, I remained impassive, my thoughts elsewhere. Finally, feeling hungry, pissed and depressed, I began the trek back to the apartment.

On my way home, my thoughts alternated between ripping Philippe out with a meat hook and using that same meat hook to teach Marie a lesson about fidelity.

The bloody thoughts triggered a memory and a beautiful song from my youth came to mind. A band called Cannibal Corpse had been around during my teenage years. Their music would be considered soft and tame by current standards, but back then they spoke to me on a level that no one else did. A tune called, *Meat Hook Sodomy* played in my head as I walked.

"I explore my thoughts through murder," said the song. I wondered if a little meat hook dentistry would do the trick with Philippe or if using the same tool to rearrange Marie's colon was the way to go. Inexplicably, the love I felt for her had quickly turned into hatred. The idea that I could bleed to death trying to detach Philippe from my gut while Marie remained unharmed and revered by throngs of fans seemed preposterous.

Remembering the song also took me back to my youth, when we had to put up with police shutting down parties and prostitution and drugs were illegal. Now I was contemplating one of the only few serious crimes left: murder.

Less than three decades earlier people had feared war, pestilence, a solar flare, the year 2012 or a nuclear holocaust while they ate their worm-burgers and sipped on their mutated-bean lattes from slightly radioactive foam cups. Few imagined that their passion for voracious, senseless consumption would do them in. Few imaged the bloody pandemonium that MegaCorp's global coup d'état brought to them in HD the second they released their trained killer biomechanical apes, mutating water viruses and mercenary humanoids. In a week they had caused government after government to fall like the powerless pricks they'd been all along. It served them right for trying to impress us with their half-assed attempts at control and regulation. Everyone knew multinational corporations owned everything, the only difference was that MegaCorp had gotten rid of pesky governments, prohibitive religions and annoying dissident groups.

Oh, what a beauty it had been to watch organic farmers being ripped in half by the powerful paws of biomechanical apes high on meth and pumped full of steroids. I had particularly enjoyed watching chai-drinking, granola-munching health nuts being decapitated and processed in order to feed MegaCorp's army of giant acidic slugs.

I had also enjoyed watching those giant slugs slither all over once-important buildings and corrode them to the ground along with the silly, worthless, flawed, unfair ideologies they contained. Those humans that survived the first onslaught actually thrived in the New World, but now I was forced to wonder if it had been worth it.

Lost in thought, I reached my street and my building. Just like that morning, piercing screams were coming from the Genital Mutilation and Erotic Maiming Center.

I stood still, enraptured by the sounds. A realization dawned on me with the force of an exploding star. Death brings new beginnings. It was a lesson everyone could learn from our New World. An end meant a beginning. The blood of politicians fertilized free thinking. The death of religion carried with it the end of war. A New World sprouted from the bloated carcass of that vile worm that had once been called democracy, in which the attainment of pleasure was an everyday occurrence. So what if we have to buy unnecessary shit? Who truly cares if what we eat and drink causes a few mutations here and there? All that death was just an introduction to new life.

In a way, homicidal thoughts were dancing in my head since the second Philippe's 9-inch snake slapped against my belly, glistening with Marie's juices in the moonlight. Those thoughts suddenly took center stage—prancing around in all their vengeful glory. A headless Marie danced naked under the rain among a forest of swaying skeletons in my head. The sheer beauty of the vision squeezed a tear from my eye.

"I'm hungry," interrupted Philippe.

"Don't fret, man, I'm going to make a little pit stop and then I'll feed you."

"Sweet, mate."

The sign on the wall read: *Genital Mutilation and Erotic Maiming Center #1143*. The place was run by my friend Screw who was somewhere in the back of the shop, mutilating someone. The screams suddenly stopped, but it was just a matter of sticking around for a few minutes and they'd start up again.

I walked to the door, yanked it open and yelled: "Hey, Screw!"

"Who goes there?"

"It's David!"

"Gutmouth! Long time no see, buddy, what can I do for you?" he called from the back.

"There's something I have to talk to you about…can we meet for a drink later?"

"Sure, man, I'll be done here at around nine."

"Same place as always?"

"Hah! You know me, Gut, I love that joint."

"See you there, bud."

I closed the door as the buzz of a power tool started and a long scream ending in laughter followed. I climbed the stairs to the apartment and had to fight four klepto roaches on the stairs. Apparently they had stolen some pills from an apartment which made them grow to about two feet long. They grabbed my right ankle and tried to pull me down. The crunch of their exoskeletons under the weight of my foot had a soothing effect on my soul. Good thing I was wearing boots.

EIGHT

While Philippe chewed and slobbered, the screams downstairs came at random intervals. They made me think about the flood of physiognomy-altering products and procedures MegaCorp had put on the market immediately after they took over. Those had truly changed humankind. The DNA-altering treatments, appendage-growing pills, interspecies skin grafts and the lifting on all bans and regulations when it came to body modifications was only the beginning. In a matter of months, biological subdermal implants and the deregulation of all genetic mutation processes turned the city into a freaky circus.

Obeying the most basic instincts of human nature, people immediately began experimenting with ways of deriving pleasure from these changes. Horse-sized penises and hairless, hypersensitive skin were just a start. As soon as people found out that a salamander DNA treatment would allow them to start regrowing a severed limb immediately after amputation, the real party began.

With this new demographic in mind, MegaCorp created a drug called Algolagnix; a yellowish serum that would turn pain into pleasure by stimulating neurological dopamine and endorphin receptors in the brain and then twisting them into a delicious knot.

The idea took off with a vengeance.

Within a year every neighborhood in town had an official MegaCorp Genital Mutilation and Erotic Maiming Center. Screw ran the one beneath my apartment—open six days a week. He and his crew also did a little tattooing, piercing and extreme body modifications such as skin grafts, sex changes, limb splitting, appendage implants, duplication, scarification, organ replacement, bone expansions, interspecies grafting and a wide array of cosmetic surgeries.

Since seeing customers leave Screw's shop in a body bag was not a strange occurrence, I made up my mind to talk to him about some safe disposal methods. Maybe I could talk Marie into trying some kinky mutilation that would just happen to go fatally wrong. It's easy to sneeze when you're using a laser or a butcher's knife. In fact, once you have someone drugged up and in a horny frenzy, the possibilities are endless.

I had an inkling that Screw could be easily convinced to help out. If the kindness of his heart faltered, there were things that could help persuade him: a night with three furry prostitutes, a date with that neighbor on the fourth floor that had the ten foot brain sticking out of her skull, a box of fuck-cakes or a trip to the private room at the Ampu-titties club for a half-hour spank session with the Colon Sisters.

If none of that worked, I could just remind him that I provided half a dozen alibis per week for him and his crew and that more than one business violation on their part had gone unpunished thanks to me. Though Tony was always the one who found someone to torture instead of Screw and the one that did all the fake paperwork.

To kill some time before the meeting with Screw, I took my pleasurebot out of the closet. It would be nice to release some of the tension that had stayed in my system from the previous night. Semen retentum venenum est!

The pleasurebot wouldn't turn on. The battery was dead. I didn't have a spare. I opened the back of the bot and pulled out the dead creature. Its limbs were muscular and grey. I didn't know why MegaCorp couldn't come up with a creature that lived a little longer.

Instead of throwing the small creature in the trash, where it would start smelling quickly, I simply left him on the floor. The klepto roaches would surely make quick work of it.

Before frustration could set in, I recalled an interactive sex book someone had given me as a birthday present. It was safely taped to some other books underneath the bed.

I walked over and pulled out the heavy package.

The title I wanted evaded me, but I remembered the author: Carlton Mellick V.

It turned out to be the fourth in the stack.

I pulled it out and taped the rest together again to keep the klepto roaches from dragging them away.

The title was, *Amazonian Sex-Assassins of the Apocalypse*. The dust jacket showed a big-breasted blonde woman wearing a loincloth. She held a bloody axe in her right hand and the head of another woman, a full-lipped brunette, in her raised left hand. The cover was appealing so I went to the index and read the names of the chapters. *Big, Sexy, Sweaty Combat* was the title of chapter four. I decided to play that one. I pressed the raised ink and set the open book on the floor.

Two huge ladies wearing nearly nothing and swinging clubs above their heads materialized. My small apartment was suddenly filled with the erotic grunts of the two babes. Their matching red manes lit the room. Despite their sexy, half-assed fight, their considerable size soon became a problem as their struggle threatened to break everything.

I stood up and closed the book. The women disappeared. Still concerned about unfulfilled needs, I turned on the computer and quickly concocted a little fantasy, emailed it and headed down to the Pregnant Purple Porpoise, a club about three blocks down from Ampu-titties.

At the club there was a group of nervous, sweaty men waiting in line outside because some tub of lard had suffered a heart attack inside. Workers were chopping him up to remove all eight hundred pounds from the cyber-encounter lounge. They fed the chunks of fat guy to a gigantic red toad with a nasty set of teeth. The toad would occasionally fart tuba notes, and puffs of blue smoke sprinkled with musical notes pooted into the air.

Finally, after the toad's tremendous feast, they vacuumed the blood and soaked the floor with disinfectant. The anxious crowd was let inside and relief shown on the face of every shifty-looking fucker in the joint.

I made my way to a booth.

A wrinkly, olive-skinned dwarf arrived with clean equipment and handed it over. The dwarf's eyes had been tattooed yellow and he had finger extensions on both hands. Each finger had three proximal phalanges instead of one, so they could bend five times. I wanted to ask him about it, but he left as soon as the equipment was out of his strange hands.

I stripped, swallowed the pill, put on all the paraphernalia, sat back down, closed my eyes and waited for the buzz.

I opened my eyes when I felt myself swinging.

A beautiful malachite sky dotted with white, spiraling clouds surrounded me. Winged beasts flew far away. When I looked up I saw the beautiful underside of a gigantic flesh dacraena draco looming above me.

Pink braided intestines filled with delicious vanilla pudding sprouted from different parts of my back and chest, keeping me airborne. The dragon tree began humming an ethereal tune and one of the flying creatures approached, right on queue.

Although the reptilian face, green skin and huge white wings did a lot for her, the woman they had assigned to the job still retained some of her features: a big, flat nose, thin lips and stringy hair. The combination was grotesque but the timer was running so I told her to pleasure me with her feet as she tore the braided intestines one by one with her fangs.

With the taste of vanilla pudding in my mouth, its refreshing coolness and delicious aroma all over my face and more of it acting as a lubricant, I felt my orgasm approaching. A small hand signal told the sex creature to cut the last of the intestines and I plunged into the endless malachite abyss. My own pudding erupted into the air and joined its sugary counterpart. There's nothing like an orgasm at zero-gravity.

A small time miscalculation meant that I ended up free-falling for a few minutes rather than the ten or twelve seconds I had expected. The experience was good, but it didn't compare to the avocado and furries episode. At that point, I was sure nothing would.

NINE

I showered as soon as I got home and then sat by the window to kill the two hours before the meeting with Screw.

As I watched the vacant street below, my mind played short movies of Marie's death. From decapitation at the hands of a skilled blind samurai from an old movie to a gruesome end at the ravenous mouths of a pack of hairless wolves that Tony kept for special occasions, each end my imagination conjured for Marie was enacted inside my head in all its gory glory. With each one came the elation one feels when a dream is about to be achieved.

The musings were interrupted twice. The first time by Philippe, who claimed he was famished. A look at the safety-fridge only produced a box of stale crackers that he wolfed down with his typical indiscrimination. The second interruption came in the stunning form of Star, the only female at Screw's shop.

She was leaving the shop in her four-legged, oxygen breathing giant Fugu fish. I called out to her and she waved back. Her long legs, which had coiling snakeskin grafts that went from her groin to her ankles, wrapped around the poisonous fish.

I stared at her long red hair, slender figure and mobile tattoos. At the sight, my broken heart began to mend. I imagined my hands playfully following her nomadic ink. *Ah, the miracle of decorated skin! The sheer beauty of an ornamented human casing!* I watched Star gallop away on her fish. I decided then and there to pursue her love as soon as the present mess was over.

When she was gone the monotonous emptiness of the street and the slowly setting sun started depressing me, so I got dressed and walked downstairs to wait for Screw at the shop.

On my way, I thought of how to ask Screw for my deadly favor without sounding like a maniac.

Halfway down the stairs, a raspy voice said "Come on, Gonzalo, mommy needs to prepare some soup." It was the small old lady that lived somewhere on the third floor. She came up the stairs very slowly, holding the banister with her right hand. She held a leash with in left hand, attached to a gigantic snail. It must have weighed fifty pounds. The old lady's hairy tail moved with a vigor that made her look younger.

I wondered what new pet scam MegaCorp had going on but decided not to ask.. The bent old woman's tail swung up every few seconds to smack at imaginary flies on her neck. I took another look at her snail and decided they were paired perfectly—both slow and ugly.

Bursting onto the street with anticipation, I threw open the door to Screw's Genital Mutilation and Erotic Maiming Center. The smell of burning flesh hung heavy in the air and the hammering beat of Screw's second CD rattled the speakers in the corners..

The song was the third track on the record, *That Weird Thing in the Gutter*. The thud of two double bass drums, or the "vicious quaternary stampede," as some critics liked to call it, sounded like a machine gun on fast-forward. The drummer, a long-haired skeleton of a man called Draggle, had four legs. All of them ended in the most impressive calves in the history of rock and roll.

In Star's absence, there was no one at the counter so I sat on a huge black leather sofa that covered half of the right wall, to wait. I thought about yelling for Screw, but the musical onslaught was restraining. I knew he wouldn't hear me.

It reminded me of the few times I had seen Assless ChaMps, Screw's postmodern zombie industrial torture rock band. The messy, violent, wild performance had only lasted about 20 minutes or so, but the aftermath of the surreal thunderstorm of sound kept my ears ringing for a week.

A huge aquarium stood against the opposite wall. Inside it, red blood cells the size of coffee plates floated around like lazy jellyfish in some transparent goo. Under the huge aquarium was a large red pillow that contained the limbless, bean-shaped body of Shrieking Jay, Screw's pet and instrument. Shrieking Jay was subjected to the vilest, most shocking and painful torture imaginable, but the guttural wails that came out of his toothless mouth were the element that really brought Screw's band together. Without his damaged vocal cords, their primal and tortured sound would be impossible.

Shrieking Jay lifted his head up a few inches to greet me, drooled a bit on his pillow, licked at the snot on his upper lip and went back to sleep.

Screw had a few more racks of flash but no new art, so the walls offered nothing new. Since there was nothing else going on, I stared at the red blood cells languidly swimming from one side of the aquarium to the other.

A faint sound came from my belly. Philippe was trying to say something. I looked down and saw my shirt moving. If he got no response, Philippe would sometimes start chewing whatever was covering him just to nag me into interacting with him. On this particular night, he could very well eat the whole shirt and go fuck himself while he was at it. I was on a mission and nothing was going to distract me.

A few minutes later the record ended and I could hear the screams of a customer. The stink of burning flesh managed to conjure up all sorts of extreme scenarios. Finally, fed up with the waiting and the smell, I got up and went into the dark hallway behind the counter.

The movement was enough to silence Philippe. The mouth was probably scared and had no idea where he was. Considering my knife antics earlier that day, he was probably thinking all kinds of crazy thoughts.

A skewed rectangle of light climbing up the wall meant that the first door on the left was halfway open. Gage's office. The stench of scorched flesh got stronger as I approached and a strange electrical hum came from beyond the door.

"Gage? You in there?"

"Is that you, Gut?" asked a voice from beyond the door.

"The one and only, baby."

"Get your ass in here, man. You don't have to wait out there all by yourself."

I pushed the door open and peeked inside.

Gage was sitting on a black stool in front of a naked man. The man was crucified to a metallic, black St. Andrew's cross; the typical X-shaped cross that every self-respecting sadomasochist has in his or her bedroom or basement dungeon.

The man's penis was covered in blood and the red mess was running down his legs. A black leather mask covered his face except for a whole that left his mouth uncovered. An intravenous drip was hooked to his left arm. The tube that went into his arm went straight to a hanging bag of Algolagnix on the other end.

I looked into Gage's only eye and smiled.

"What are you up to, Titface?" I asked while looking at the lily-white, dark-nippled breast that sprouted from the left side of Gage's face.

"Not much, man. I'm almost done with this guy. You here to see Screw?"

"Yeah. Is he around?"

"He's working on a lady right now. Take a seat over there and I'll be with you in a minute." Gage pointed to a stool in the corner of room. It was next to another aquarium. Instead of water, this one contained about a foot of a gelatinous substance that quivered constantly like a flan in the hand of a Parkinson's patient.

"Hey, Boobface, what's in the aquarium?"

"Platelets," replied Gage without looking away from the man's penis. "It's a new safety regulation. We had a few hemophiliacs who didn't say shit when they filled out their papers and... well, now every center has to have one of those."

"Why not just let the dishonest assholes die?"

"Because if we do, then we have to clean up all the blood and fill a ton of paperwork."

"Hmm. Makes sense."

Gage didn't reply. I sat down and watched the artist work.

He had the crucified man's penis in his hand. Well, one side of it. Apparently he was using a small laser to split the thing in half. I wondered how he managed not to botch such a delicate job with the messed depth of perception that comes with having only one eye.

The electric hum came back and Gage applied the cauterizing instrument to the man's half-split unit. The guy started screaming again. At the end of every howl, a smile crossed his lips. The bifurcated dick twitched in a silly attempt at becoming erect while gushing blood. Just then, a spurt of blood flew over Gage's head and landed behind him. A quick flick of the humming/splitting apparatus and the blood squirting was over.

I couldn't stomach much more so I looked at Gage's left arm. In order to maintain artistic symmetry, Gage had covered his left arm with human nipples from wrist to shoulder. Just like in the real world, the nipples ran the gamut when it came to color, width, species and length. Some of them even sported shiny stubs or gold hoops.

The next few minutes were more of the same. Finally, the splitting was done. Gage disinfected the two halves and coated them with a liquid plastic that was protective, adhesive and antibacterial. Then he released the guy and removed the leather mask.

"How are you feeling?" Gage cleaned his equipment, wiping up blood.

"I feel alive!" said the man. "That was the most exhilarating experience of my life!"

"Yeah, I know. I would put it somewhere above bungee jumping and below raping a biomechanical gorilla."

"Fuck bungee jumping, bro! This is the real deal!"

"Glad to know you're happy," said Gage with a slightly dismissive tone.

"What do I owe you?" asked the man while he walked to the corner and picked up his clothes.

"It'll be a hundred. And remember: no long baths, no playing with it for a while and no scratching the plastic off because, if you do, it will heal all wrong and the two halves will try to stick together, got it?"

"Sure. Here you go." The semi-dressed man handed Gage a few bills, stepped into his pants, picked up his shoes and walked out buttoning his shirt with one hand. It seemed like he was in a hurry to get home and be alone with his new toy.

"So what's up, Gut?"

"Not much, Gage. You do a lot of those?" I asked pointing at the empty doorway.

"Penis splits? Sure. I guess the shop as a whole does about ten or twelve a week."

"Looks painful."

"You bet your ass it's painful. That's why they do it. Your tool is chuck-full of nerve endings; more than you can imagine. You see that little bag up there?"

"The Algolagnix? Sure. Does it really work?"

"Like nobody's business. They get a few drops of that in their system and you can hack off their legs with a blunt hatchet covered in salt and they would laugh and ask for more."

"But that dude was screaming."

"They all scream. It's some sort of weird psychological reaction, you know?" explained Gage. "Since they know it's supposed to hurt they imagine the pain, but what they really feel is the pleasure. Their receptors are all fucking tied in a confused knot. They scream out of fear or confusion or imagined pain or whatever the hell is going on in these fuckers' sick heads."

"If you say so."

"Gut, I've seen people bleed to death while asking for more. I've had clients that ask me to cut off all their limbs in a single session. Shit, I had a woman in here last week that wanted me to imbed a bunch of small nails all over her body so that every movement she made would send her into a pleasure whirl. Said she got the idea from some guy at the Church of Albert Fish."

"Did you do it?"

"Hell no, you can only keep someone going on Algolagnix for a few hours and then you have to stop, otherwise their

51

brain shuts down. If I had done it, she would've passed out from the pain the second the Algolagnix wore off."

"Interesting job you have."

"Yeah, it sure beats flipping synthetic burgers for a living."

"I bet it does," I said. "Hey, how long do you think whatever Screw is doing is going to take?"

"Let me finish here and I'll take you there. He should be just about done."

"Do your thing."

I stepped out of Gage's office and waited for him with my back against the wall. Screw's door was barely distinguishable at the end of the hallway. All the information Gage had given me had me wondering about what the best approach would be for what I had in mind.

I could try to convince Marie of doing something ordinary like a bit of nipple torture or maybe a bit of cutting, maybe even a finger, but she would never go for the hardcore maiming stuff. Plus, that would only happen after she underwent a salamander DNA treatment. Those were the rules. If she did that, it would bring back her leg, which was something she would never allow to happen. Also, kinky as she was, she disliked the sight of blood. Even if she eventually agreed to undergo the treatment, the experience of losing her leg had most likely traumatized her. I didn't think she would even discuss erotic amputation.

Then I thought maybe I could use that bit about the nerve endings to convince her of some genital punishment experimentation. Screw could just mistakenly allow her to stay on the Algolagnix for too long...

Gage came out of the room with a small backpack in his left hand and a set of keys in the other. He closed his door and turned to me.

"Did I tell you I finished Amanda?"

Amanda was one of Gage's ex-girlfriends. He had agreed to help her out with one of her radical body art performances.

"No, you never told me. Is she happy with the outcome?"

"I don't think so. We found out after we were almost done that there was no way to cram her larynx anywhere on the body."

"Meaning?"

"Meaning I don't know whether she likes it or not because she has no voice. Her lips, tongue, larynx, vocal cords, teeth, lungs, stomach, kidneys and other bits and pieces are in my freezer at home."

"Hold on just a minute; how does she breathe if she has no lungs?"

"She doesn't. The serum I give her keeps the tissues oxygenated. You have to remember this was an experiment and at some point we're going to put her back together. Right now we are just using the parts that we need like the skin, eyes, hair, most of the bones, fingers... that kind of thing."

"And when will you put her back together?" I asked, trying hard to grasp the extent of what the man with the boob on his face was saying.

"I don't know. The thing is that it all worked great on paper but we don't know how to reactivate the circulatory system or how to remake a bunch of other things we chopped up, destroyed or simply lost during the process."

"Can't you do it with electricity? Shock the heart to make it start pumping again?" I remembered a few classes here and there.

"The heart pumps just fine, but for the whole thing to work first we have to put all the veins back into place and... it's just a mess and a lot of work."

"Well, that sucks."

"Yeah. Come on, I'll show her to you."

As we walked, Gage's face-breast bounced up and down just like a normal breast would.

"Hey, Gage," I said pointing at his face. "You ever thought about giving that thing some tan lines?"

Gage's elbow hit me right on the ribs. I doubled over and clutched my side in pain. He said, "Maybe you should pimp out that thing you have on your gut. I bet you could teach it how to give blowjobs to truck drivers for ten bucks a pop."

"Listen, you bloody cunt, why don't you go sit on some trucker's face and tell him all about your brilliant ideas?" Philippe chimed in.

"Hah! I'd never heard that abomination talk before!"

"Abomination strikes me as a bit of a heavy word for a man who's currently depriving some village of an idiot." Retorted the mouth.

"Wow, Gut, he's witty, too. You sure you don't want me or Screw to try to sew him shut?"

"Feel free to address me, you inconsiderate hog. I'm the one you're talking to," said Philippe before I could reply.

"Tell that thing to shut the hell up, man."

"Philippe, be quiet for a while," I said.

"All you ask me is to be quite," whined Philippe. "Maybe you should be quiet for a while. Maybe I'm tired of listening to you. Maybe…"

With one quick motion, Gage stuffed a corner of his rucksack into Philippe. It surprised the hell out of me, but it got the job done. When Gage removed the rucksack, the mouth remained quiet.

"Glad that worked," said Gage. "I don't know how you can deal with that blabbing thing everyday."

"Sometimes I ask myself that same question," I replied, still clutching my ribs.

Gage shook his head and the tip of the nipple swung from left to right in an arc that almost hit the right side of his face. I followed him down the hall.

Almost at the end of the hallway, about five feet from Screw's closed door, Gage unlocked a door on the left and popped on the light. The flash of bulbs were blinding, but our eyes adjusted as we went inside.

With a sweep of his arm, Gage introduced his magnum opus. "What do you think, Gut? Pretty cool, isn't she?"

All of their previous conversations had done nothing to prepare me for what I saw. By some unimaginable rearrangement of bones and other bodily materials, Amanda was a bicycle. Thousands of stitches crisscrossed her twisted body. Tubes protruded from her thin frame in odd places. Amanda, a woman I had once known, was now an atrocity wrapped in artistic intent and propped against a dirty wall.

"She thought people would immediately get the innuendo, you know? Go for a ride, ride a girl, etcetera," said Gage.

"She's... she's a fucking bicycle!" was all I could say, feeling simultaneously fascinated and repulsed.

"Yeah, it took me almost two months but she's all done," said Gage, his voice filled with pride. "She's so well put together that you can even take her out for a ride."

"Are you serious?"

"Hell yeah, man, the only thing that I would change is that I have to bring her back here every three or four hours to oxygenate the tissue or it'll start to rot. Other than that, she runs like a dream. Look at the thick wheels I put on her. I've been thinking about using some of the leftover bones to make some rims."

Gage explained that the small box in front of Amanda's front wheel pumped liquid that oxygenated her skin. Her two plump butt cheeks served as the seat and her arms were twisted to make the shape of the handle. The frame itself was a collection of irregular bits and pieces. Most of it came from her legs, but Gage had used many parts to build the rest.

Amanda's boobs hung from the top tube, one near the head tube and the other almost under the seat. Stainless steel rings hung from both nipples. On top of the down tube, her ten toes were sewn in from largest to smallest, giving the impression of a stubby crest. The chain was made from her smaller vertebrae and some tiny bones I guessed came from her fingers. The peddles were her scapulas. Finally, on a small fleshy panel stuck between the handles, right where the reflective light should've been, a pair of bleary red eyes stared back at us.

"She looks good to me," I lied, trying to ignore a small twitch on one of her fingers. "What are you guys going to do next?"

"Well, I don't know. Amanda originally wanted to do this in order to enter some competition but I'm pretty sure we missed the deadline. At some point I'll get around to creating a voice box for her and then maybe I can get her to talk. It'd be pretty cool to get her into some sort of show, you know? Get her someplace where people get to see her and appreciate what we have done."

I couldn't help stealing a few more glances at the bike as

Gage talked and then a few more when he did a little motion with his chin that signaled the end of the conversation and made the boob on his face jiggle yet again. My mind was officially blown.

We started to walk to the door and I looked at the Amandacycle one last time. Tears were filling the groggy pair of eyes between the handles. With my back to it and a creeping sensation clawing at the back of my legs, I was glad to leave the room.

Gage locked the door behind him and we walked to Screw's office.

Gage knocked a few times and a voice screamed from inside.

"That you, Gage?"

"Yeah, man, I'm here with Gut."

A few seconds went by and then the door creaked open.

Screw stood there, tall and rail-thin. The smile on his lips fully displayed his metal teeth. The multihued silicon spikes sprouting from the top of his brow and ending at the nape of his neck gave him a perennial Mohawk. He was wearing elbow-high black latex gloves. His exposed biceps and shoulders were covered with colorful, moving tattoos. A bug-eyed koi fish swam against the current in a blue river on his left arm as a few cherry blossom flowers spun wildly on top of the water. On his right arm, a series of tribal designs rearranged their pattern constantly while humming an almost imperceptible tune. His black, sleeveless shirt read "Rutger Hauer is fucking God!" in blocky white letters.

"Gut, my friend, always the impatient one," said Screw.

"Good to see you, Screw. You busy?"

"I'm almost done. Come in."

"Actually, I'm heading out," said Gage. "I have a client that wants me to make a house call. She wants a Persian cat skin graft on her back."

"Alright, Gage, Just make sure you bring your shit back clean," said Screw pointing at the backpack.

"Will do. Wish me luck; I hope to be balls deep in her honeypot before the stroke of midnight."

"Good luck," I said.

Screw just looked at him and shook his head. "Take a seat over there, Gut. I'll be with you in a minute and we can get the hell out of here."

Gage patted me on the back and left. I stepped into Screw's office and shut the door behind me.

There was a table in the middle of the room. A chubby woman was spread-eagled face-down across it, held down by a strange metal contraption that resembled a big saddle with spider legs. Her reddish skin tone meant she probably had some demon blood. She was facing the door and her long black hair cascaded all the way to the floor. Her gigantic, pendulous breasts seemed to be caressing the table underneath her.

I moved to sit in the plastic chair in the corner and noticed something behind her. I made it to the chair and could see that there was a muscular, skinned animal halfway up the woman's rectum. There were cables attached to the legs of the creature with a bulky mess of electrical tape. They led to a small box on the floor with buttons on it.

Screw stood beside the box, bent down and pushed a button. The skinned, rabbit-like creature started flopping and jumping so hard I was sure it would fly out of the woman's ass, or rip her to shreds trying. But neither happened. Instead, the plump lady began squirming and moaning.

The moaning mayhem was over in about five minutes. Screw pushed another button and there was a slurping sound followed by a loud, wet thud as the thing slid out of her butthole. The rabbit thing just lay on the floor, huge and lifeless. It had a human face. I mumbled something about having to take a leak and stepped out.

The chunky demon chick came out of Screw's office after a couple of minutes. Nothing in her ponytail, beige pant suit or thick-rimmed glasses hinted at what she had just enjoyed. Since I was standing beside the door, I opened it for her. She smiled at me with the sweetest, friendliest smile I had seen in a long time. As she walked past me, her scent wafted to my nose. She smelled like angel farts ought to smell.

TEN

Screw came out, and I noticed he'd changed his shirt to one with one of those bullet-hole smiley faces on it. We locked the shop and began the six block trip to the bar.

It was a quarter past nine. Darkness enveloped the city and the few working street lights only managed to fully illuminate the gigantic asses that hovered above the sidewalks.

The city always struck me as a huge disaster waiting to happen, a tightly coiled spring of death ready to pop, a cosmic jack-in-the-box of mayhem, a Pandora's Box of pestilence and blood, a fucking piñata of dangerous lunatics that is broken by the stick of night. Now, walking to a bar to plan a murder, I began to understand why violence is so common.

Since MegaCorp became God, the night was filled with maimed and mutated creatures swarming the city's hot, gloomy streets like misshapen mosquitoes on a fetid concrete mangrove.

Screw and I walked in silence. We passed a few piles of unpicked garbage bags that offered a great meal opportunity for many a nighttime creature.

When walking alone, I would sometimes stop to look at the remains of those nasty bags. They were like a repulsive addendum to life in the city. I always thought the garbage spoke volumes about what goes on behind the closed doors. On any given day I could come across used needles, broken glass, overloaded diapers, empty bottles of cheap booze, dead creatures of all sizes, fire-stained pieces of aluminum foil, sticky porn magazines, unopened envelopes containing MegaCorp bills, demon fetuses, pregnancy tests (both crushingly positive and mercifully negative), crumpled endorphinated beer cans, empty pill bottles, bloody clothing, used toilette paper, guts, unidentifiable flesh fragments, packages of microwaveable or self-heating dinners, broken computers, dead furries, soiled underwear…. the detritus of a cesspool.

After a few piles of garbage and one undead addict vomiting on his own chest, Screw and I reached the Monocotyledonous, a greasy joint that played the kind of music we both enjoyed and served cheap, powerful drinks that got folks savagely drunk on a budget. Its neon sign consisted of its long name and an unrecognizable bunch of twisting lines over it that were supposed to look like an exotic flower but instead looked like a bunch of worms fighting a dozen shoelaces.

We walked in and ordered a few endorphinated beers. We took a seat near the door. The joint was a long corridor that must've been about ten or twelve feet across and had no air conditioning and no windows. At some point before MegaCorp came along and enforced the use of their too-expensive vehicles on everyone, it had been a two-car garage.

Screw and I picked a spot as close as possible to the door in a fruitless attempt to escape the heat inside and the offensive odors of the patrons. Our attempt at getting some fresh air collided with the putrid smells coming from the gutter.

My nerves were almost fried and Screw kept the silence from becoming awkward by engaging in small talk. A few nods and a couple of monosyllabic answers almost made me look like an active part of the conversation. I was trying to mentally escape the stench-sandwich by entertaining other senses. I tapped my fingers continuously on the cold can in my hand and my eyes were glued to the huge woman behind the bar.

She was dancing by herself while serving the few customers that were brave enough to put up with the stifling heat and dreadful smell inside. Not much of her horrendous anatomy was left to the imagination. A tight pair of low-riding jeans were topped with a roll of stretch-marked fat and her thin, black spandex sports-bra couldn't quite contain her massive fat-pocked breasts. The stub of a single horn sprouted from her left temple.

Sweat poured from her round body. Beads of salty skin water glistened under neon lights, giving her an alternating greenish-reddish glow. She looked radioactive. I was sure her kiss was more dangerous than a plutonium bath.

I was looking at her and vaguely smiling any time she looked my way. It wasn't that I liked her. In fact, she scared me more than any of the other alcohol-fueled lowlifes in the place. It was that on top of the greenish glow and the jerky alien dancing, she had a lazy eye. Her left eye seemed to be either watching out for airplanes inside the bar or scanning the floor for loose change. I'm a cruel bastard, but I found the whole thing funny as hell. As if that wasn't enough, Tony and his appreciation for women kept popping into my head. Some of the names he usually used seemed to fit this blob perfectly: porky, lardo, whale, elephantine, chank, heifer, hog, obeast, fucking yak...

She would also wipe herself off a bit with each napkin before wrapping it around the bottom of every endorphinated beer or hallucinatory drink she served. Other people had noticed too, but nobody said a thing. When people end up hanging out at a place like this and paying next to nothing for their drinks, nobody bitches about a sweaty napkin. As I was enjoying another swipe-and-wrap maneuver from the dancing Queen of Cellulite, Screw broke whatever bullshit silence thing we had going on.

"Why are we here Gut?"

"What?"

"We have a beer three or four times a year and it's usually someone's birthday or something. Today you come looking for me, bring me here and then stare at that blob behind the bar instead of talking to me. Wouldn't you agree something's up?"

"You're right Screw. I brought you here because I need your help."

A smile slowly curled the sides of Screw's mouth up and the metallic teeth reflected the flashes of red and green that came from the overhead lights.

"That's more like it. What can I do for you?"

"Well… it's not an everyday favor. What I need is kind of… I guess you could say it's a matter of life and death."

"Come on, man, you've saved my ass more times than I can count and

"Listen, Screw, I need to get rid of Marie," the words left my mouth before I could process them. Apparently my subconscious had already decided not to sugarcoat the whole mess.

"What are you talking about man?" asked Screw with a playful smirk on his face. "Do you have her body stuffed under your bed or do you want some relationship advice?"

"I want to see how you handle this, you barmpot," said Philippe. Thankfully, his voice was muffled by the shirt that covered him.

"Did that toothed hole just say something?" asked Screw.

"Forget about him," I replied almost whispering and suddenly paranoid about discussing Marie's death in a public space. "The point is that Marie needs to be… dealt with."

"Dealt with?"

I leaned over the table as far as my gut would allow. "I need to kill her, Screw."

"Are you serious? I'm in no mood for sick jokes. I had a long day."

"I'm dead fucking serious."

Philippe chuckled audibly.

Screw leaned in a few inches. "And what do you want me to help you with?"

"I thought maybe I could bring her to the shop for something and then…you know, whatever she decides to get done can go horribly wrong."

"You can't be fucking serious," said Screw.

Philippe mumbled something.

"No, man, this is no joke. The only way…"

"Listen, Gut, I really don't know what you want me to do for you but, I can't help you kill Marie," said Screw.

"I see clients leave your shop in body bags every week…"

"You do, but they are hardcore freaks, hemophiliacs that

lied on their paperwork, weirdoes that showed up high on something that reacted bad with the Algolagnix…I mean, the thing is there's a lot of paperwork and sometimes MegaCorp will come by and investigate shit if they're not happy with our report, you know better than anybody how they hate to lose paying customers."

"Yeah," was all I could muster.

"What I'm trying to say is that it's not that easy, Gut. I know we don't have to put up with the police anymore, but that doesn't mean there's no bureaucracy, you know what I'm saying?"

"I know, Screw, don't worry about it. Forget I even asked you, man, I don't know what got into me."

"Breakups can be a bitch, Gut. Listen, I have some pills that'll help."

"Don't worry about it, Screw. Seriously." I stood and gave Screw a pat of the shoulder. Screw's metallic teeth glinted in the night. "I'm going to hit the sack. I'll talk to you later."

I went home and climbed the stairs to my apartment. I heard klepto roaches scurrying to distant corners, dragging stolen things.

I took my shoes off, tied them down to the coffee table and climbed into bed. My resolution to kill Marie was now shaky.

"You need to kill that trollop, mate. If you don't, she's going to make a nutter out of you," said Philippe.

"How the fuck did you know what I was thinking about?"

"I'm part of you, mate, I don't need to read your thoughts to know what's on your mind."

"I'm going to sleep now. We can talk about it in the morning."

"No problem. Can we get something to eat first?"

I grabbed the gun that was still wedged in my pants and stuck the barrel inside Philippe. I'd taken my gun before leaving the house, and now it was serving a purpose. The mouth mumbled something and I removed the gun.

"I get your point, you bloody whacko. Good night."

I didn't reply. Somewhere in the distance a man kept

screaming "No, don't do it!" Fortunately, I didn't believe in omens.

My eyes felt heavy. I was asleep before my head hit the pillow Velcroed to my bed.

That night, I didn't dream. If I'd know then that my life would take such and awful turn that my ass would end up in prison, I probably would have eaten a bullet or taken enough pills to ensure there would be no waking up. However, Philippe had me convinced getting rid of Marie was the way to go.

ELEVEN

On my third day in prison I got a visit from Tony. I was awake and Philippe was finishing the last of the purple porridge when the smelly guard brought Tony over to the cell. Tony was a tad shorter than the guard but considerably wider. It was obvious that the guard felt uncomfortable with the situation.

"You have a vissssssssitor," said the squid.

"Let him in and go get us some coffee, Stinky."

The guard didn't reply.

The door swung open and Tony's hulking figure stepped into the cell. He looked around and poked the wall a few times with his fingers.

"Cozy place you got here, Gut."

"I've had worse. At least there's no klepto cockroaches."

"I hear you," said Tony. He sat beside me on my cot. "How you holding up?"

"I've been better."

"Yeah, I guess death row is a bitch, ain't it?"

"More or less."

"Listen," said the rat while looking toward the door. "Screw came by the Rehab Center yesterday."

"And?"

"And he was feeling bad about not helping you out."

"Well, tell him not to worry about it."

"I told him about Philippe and Marie and he realized you had your reasons to get rid of her," said Tony. His protuberant nose twitched.

"I would appreciate if you didn't talk about me behind my back, you filthy rodent," said Philippe.

"I'm not here to talk to you, you toothy fuck," replied

64

Tony.

I couldn't handle an argument between the mouth and the rat just then, so I interrupted. "Thanks for coming Tony. I missed seeing a familiar face."

"Don't mention it. I feel a little responsible,,, You know. Oh, Bella sends you a bunch of kisses," the rodent said with a smile.

"You can keep them."

"I gotta go, Gut, but I'll see you soon, alright?"

"Wait. What? You came here just to tell me Screw is feeling bad about not helping me?"

"Pretty much. And I wanted to check out your digs." Tony stood.

"Okay. Great. Thanks."

Tony called for the guard. Then he turned to me. "I don't know how you can stand that fuckin' mouth on your stomach. He reeks of chum."

"I know," I replied. "Hey, Tony, you think you can try to figure out when they're going to kill me?"

"I'll come back soon, and I'll try and find out."

"Thanks, man, I appreciate it."

The hissing squid showed up and opened the door. Tony looked him up and down. "Despite what they might've told you, breath mints are not poisonous."

"That'sssssssss very funny coming from a hairy dissssssseasssssssse carrier sssssssuch assssssss yourssssssself."

"If I gave you leptospirosis I don't know what would be more painful for you—the symptoms from it or having to say it," said Tony.

I laughed and even Philippe chuckled. The security squid led the bodybuilding rat down the corridor. I sat alone and pondered the laughs I would never get to have with Tony, Bella, Screw, Gage, Star or anybody else again.

The two remaining acidophilus bacteria swam in the toilet. Shitting in my hand and then sitting there and waiting for the guard to pass struck me as a constructive way of spending the next hour or so. The only good thing about facing death is that you learn to appreciate life's little pleasures.

TWELVE

Tony's visit cheered me up a bit. The rat was a real friend. Even feeling guilty, he came to see me. If only briefly. I thought it might even be a little risky for him. I was happy to see he hadn't been implicated in my crime.

After Screw shut down my first plan of action, I decided to take care of business myself. In order to do that, I required something not available to the general public. Namely, one of the special guns used at the Customer Rehabilitation Center. Why? Because a simple bullet from a .38 would be too crass and impersonal. Furthermore, it would also be easily tracked back to me and, last but not least, it would leave the problem of a bleeding one-legged corpse to deal with.

So a few days after Screw said no way, I had a new plan. I nestled the gun between my jeans and lower back and dropped by the office after my first text came. It was 9:20 AM. It seemed like people couldn't get up fast enough to start doing shit that went against MegaCorp regulations.

The address was almost out of my area. I hopped on my car and drove for about twenty minutes with the GPS cussing at me for missing exits over and over again.

I finally reached a dilapidated building smack in the middle of what used to be the meat-packing district. Someone had reported a small group of individuals living there instead of paying rent to MegaCorp like the rest of the world.

I parked in front of the ramshackle building and approached it with the healthy dose of trepidation that every hunter should use to keep him hyperaware. I heard the sound of something heavy being dragged a few floors above me as I reached the doorway. I entered the place with gun in hand and slowly checked out the first floor.

The only thing I found was a circular patch of yellow fungus growing on one of the bathroom walls that seemed to be whispering something. I got close to it and heard indistinct voices coming from it. I got my ass out of there quickly.

The second floor was also empty except for a few discarded items of clothing, some rotting furniture and a pile of rusty home appliances. The dragging sound seemed to be coming from the top floor, just above me. As I neared the stairs at the end of the hall, I noticed a transparent, viscous substance slowly dripping from the ceiling and making a clear puddle on the floor. I hesitated to climb to the third floor. The dragging noises were certainly coming from there and whatever was making them was either very heavy or strong enough to drag something very heavy around. Neither of those possibilities pleased me. I took a deep breath and climbed the rickety stairs trying to make as little noise as possible.

The morning sun was coming through the windows and the whole place was inundated with the sort of daylight that normally keeps fears of dark things at bay. I tried to concentrate on the light but still felt a bit scared. Walking across the threshold, I entered a big room. It was empty. I walked down the corridor at the far end of the room.

I entered a second room which held the first nasty surprise of the day. A small, black, bony creature no taller than a dwarf was standing in a corner. It faced the wall, shaking. Small, membranous, bat wings ran down its back.

I slowly approached with the gun trained on it. I heard something scurry behind me and turned just in time to see another one of those things crawling toward my legs. The bat-thing shrieked when I shot it and reached forward with its scrawny arm. My second shot blew off the top of its nasty little head.

Turning, I found that the other creature had disappeared from the corner. A flapping noise came from somewhere above my head. I looked up just as the thing came diving straight at my face. This time a single shot did the trick and the thing landed on the floor with a loud thud. I pinned the wriggling thing to the floor with my boot to get a good look at it.

There was a tiny human hand at the end of each wing.

Then the creature spoke. "Fuck you."

I jumped back instinctively and, immediately ashamed of the girly reaction, put a bullet through one the thing's shark eyes.

I scanned the room and found no freaky creatures. I slowly made my way through the rest of the rooms. There was nothing in the next two rooms, but the third room was occupied.

The dragging sound reached my ears before I could see into the room. It sounded like a blubbery chunk of dead whale being dragged over a wooden floor. I jumped in front of the door with the gun ready and my heart hammering.

A massive white worm with the torso of a woman was slowly making its way from one side of the room to the other. It was completely bald and its engorged breasts were oozing a brown liquid that ran all the way down to the floor. The thing stopped moving and turned to the door. I noticed she had a bottle of wine in her right hand.

"Nihilism I tell you," said the worm-woman with a voice that sounded like it was coming from an underwater source a few countries away.

"Can you understand me?" I asked, trying to keep my voice steady.

"NOTHING! No way out! Emptiness! Endless voids of zilch! NOTHING!" The maggot-woman stared at me with panicked eyes and smashed the bottle against the wall. She picked up one of the larger pieces of glass, and sliced her throat from ear to ear. By the time the blood splattered on the floor, I was out the door.

I had to file a report at the Rehabilitation Center detailing what had gone down and saying that no one, or no thing capable of paying rent, was living at the crumbling building anymore.

Tony was pouring lacquer thinner down a guy's wrecked back and ass when I walked in. The poor bastard was in thumbscrews tied to a chain hanging from the ceiling. Every muscle in his naked body was stretched to the snapping point but no sounds came from his mouth.

"Hey Tony, how's it going?"

"Not bad, Gut. You?"

"Ah, just finished checking out a report of some squatters."

"You brought anybody in?"

"Nah, it wasn't exactly what I was expecting."

"Bummer, Bella hooked me up with a little device I'm trying out that keeps the screaming to a minimum."

"Yeah? What is it?"

"Check this dude's neck out," said the rat with a smile.

The man was wearing a heretic's fork. A long metallic rod with split, sharpened ends was wedged between his lower jaw and sternum. His head was thrown back and any opening of the mouth would simultaneously drive the sharp ends of the fork into his chest and chin. His face was contorted and snot and tears were running down his face and neck.

"Bella is sick, man. Where the hell did she get this thing?" I asked.

"According to Bella, one of her lovers died of a heart attack. She was the one that found him so she took a few things from his apartment before calling the Inquiry and Disposal team. She also showed me a wooden thing that looked like a vise with rusty spikes on both sides. She's having it cleaned and plans to use it to put some guy's balls in it and crush them very slowly."

"That's not a nice picture, but thank you for the information."

"You're welcome." Tony whipped the man some more.

"What did this guy do?"

"Parrot brought him in. You know Parrot right? The guy with no nose?"

"Yeah."

"Well, he brought him in. Apparently this fellow thought it'd be a good idea to walk into a MegaStore, fill his pockets with canned fetus strips and walk out without paying."

"What's all this fetus meat crap? They're serving that shit everywhere now."

"Yeah, it's the softest, sweetest meat you can get," explained Tony. "It's very high in protein, too. MegaCorp is producing the stuff in China because they have way more women to work with over there. Anyway, there's a taco stand about…"

"Yeah, I've been there. Good stuff."

"Exactly my point," said Tony and he put the whip down and poured some more thinner on the guy's back. While he hadn't really moved all that much during the whipping, the prisoner now tensed again, veins popping all over his skinny body, and grunted like a feral hog.

"Hey, Tony, there's something I need to talk to you about when you get a second."

"You want to go outside right now? I'm sort of tired of going at this dude's back."

"Sure thing," I replied.

Tony slapped the guy's bloody ass and promised to be right back with a wink.

We stepped out into the hallway and I told him all that had gone down between Marie and Philippe. I asked for his help and told Tony to feel free to say no as Screw had already done so and the least thing I wanted was to have him lose his job.

Tony listened intently, nodding once in a while and shaking his head a few times. His massive, hairy chest puffed out and he let it go with an audible sigh when I was done. Philippe remained mercifully quiet for the duration of our conversation.

"You need to do whatever you think you need to do," said Tony once I was done talking. "What I want to know is what you want me to do."

"You know what? I'm not sure," I confessed. "I thought about a few ways of making Marie break a regulation and then bring her here, but that would entail reviving our relationship. I guess I'm asking for your help because I don't know what to do."

"You're in luck, my friend. I think I know how you can take care of this issue pronto."

"I'm all ears."

"You know I fucking hate ear jokes, Gut."

"My bad. It slipped out."

"Right," he said looking around. "Follow me."

Without another word, Tony began walking down the hallway. I hurried to keep up with his long strides. At the end of the hall, Tony pulled a card out of his pocket and swept it through a slot on top of a black box. The door buzzed open and we stepped through. A long corridor with bad lighting stretched in front of us. We began walking again and soon came to a cell. I realized this was the place they used to hold the prisoners that awaited torture.

The guy in the first cell was naked and curled up on the bare concrete floor with his back toward the door. His exposed spine seemed to be painted like a child's xylophone.

The second cell contained a willowy woman with long blonde hair, a tattered green dress and a considerable skin flap hanging from her bloody forehead. She was standing on a corner and appeared to be mumbling to herself.

There was a naked fat guy in the third cell with incredibly thick glasses and no teeth. Drool slid from his gaping mouth as he masturbated. He went at it so fast and furiously that I thought he'd pull off his dick.

Tony said, "We're gonna pay my friend Loo a little visit."

"Who's Loo?" It was the first time I had heard the name.

"He's the man in charge of special torturing and disposal tools."

"Great. Is he the guy responsible for the hatchets, thick garbage bags, gasoline, acid, pliers and all that other stuff?"

"When was the last time you were here for a disposal?"

"I don't know. A year?"

"Sounds more like a decade to me. We have more recent tools that make the whole process a little cleaner and faster."

"Sounds good to me."

We kept walking in silence. I turned just in time to see the guy in the last cell. He was sitting in the middle of the cell facing the door. He had no arms and the fresh stumps dripped with pus. He had dead eyes.

"Whet the hell happened to this guy?" I had to ask.

"Fuck, Gut, you ask a lot of damn questions, man! I don't know. The pervert showed up with no arms. He's going leave this place with no balls, you think I care? I'll drag him in later and let Bella take care of business with her

71

new toy and the rest of the story is not my fucking business. It's that simple."

"That's great, but he never raped the bot."

"What do you mean?"

"He used a piece of it to scratch his belly button from the inside; that's not raping the pleasurebot." Nerves were apparently turning me into a stickler for regulations.

"We couldn't care less, Gut. If you want I can call the boss and you can defend the guy."

"No, that's okay."

"Yeah, that's what I though."

The corridor finally reached an end and Tony pushed open another door. We entered a small room with two low-wattage bulbs hanging from the ceiling. A fence with a small opening filled the entire left side of the room. A guy with thick grey tubes coming out of his nostrils smiled at us with teeth so big and crooked he looked like something pulled from a horror flick. .

"Big T!" The man's voice was artificial and sounded like slowed down audio.

"How you doing, Loo?"

"Not bad, not bad. What brings you to the dungeon?"

"I'm done with my guy and I need one of the new puddle-makers."

Loo looked at Tony and then at me. He then lowered his eyes and scanned a document he had on the table in front of him.

"You mean the fetus muncher?"

"That's him."

"Well, he's not scheduled for disposal, T," Loo said looking at both of us with obvious suspicion creeping into his fake voice.

"Listen, Loo," said Tony approaching the cage. The rat held on to the mesh as high as his muscular arms allowed. "This is a special favor you're doing me here, buddy."

"You know the regulations, T, I can't just give you the equipment without the proper paperwork." The tubed man's mechanical voice cracked.

Screw had mentioned paperwork and now Loo was

throwing a wrench in whatever plan Tony had concocted with the paperwork thing once again. It made me realize that the disappearance of one form of oppressive power does not mean the end of fucking official procedures. It was painful to remember what I had known since MegaCorp came to power—hegemony is like energy. It can be transformed, but never destroyed.

"Sure you can, Loo. You're the man here! Whatever you say goes. It'll only take an hour or so."

"Who's him?" Loo asked looking at me.

"A good friend of mine. He's in a bind, Loo. He's a MegaCorp hunter and he needs our help, man. Are you really going to leave us hanging?"

"If I give it to you and they trace it back to me…"

"It won't happen," interrupted Tony. "You'll have the thing back in an hour and no one will be the wiser, deal?"

"I just can't…"

Tony rattled the fence a bit and Loo jumped out of his seat.

"Be a fucking buddy, Loo. I'll hook you up with that wrestler chick I told you about. She can squeeze your melon between her legs until you pass out."

Loo said nothing but nodded twice and disappeared into the gloom that opened up behind the fence. Tony looked at me and winked. A minute later Loo came back with a small black box that resembled a camera case and handed it to Tony.

"Bring it back quickly, T. I'll deny the whole thing and have you fired if anything comes back to me."

"You got it, Loo. I owe you one. I'll make sure Droka breaks your dick in half, bud."

Loo smiled, flashing those horror-teeth again. Tony walked back to the door and we hurried down the dim corridor without a word.

Back in the torture chamber, Tony closed the door. The guy tied to the ceiling had passed out. The stench of feces, coagulated blood, piss, snot and lacquer thinner was overpowering. Tony opened the small case and handed me a small rectangular thing.

It felt like cheap plastic. Tony told me to make sure the safety was on at all times and only take it off to fire one shot at Marie and then put it immediately back on.

I told him I had a gun and was about to ask him what was so special about this one when he said "This is not a gun, Gut, it's something more. Shoot it one time and get the hell away. Don't let anyone see it. Bring it back as soon as you're done. You need to get out of here now and take care of business. This is serious, Gut. Being fired is the least of my worries if someone finds out I let you have this."

"No need to worry, man," I said. "I know you're sticking your neck out there for me, so letting you down is not an option. I'll follow your instructions and head back here immediately. I give you my word on that."

I thanked him and left.

I hopped on the car and looked at my watch. It was ten past noon. Ampu-titties opened at eleven so at that hour Marie was probably pleasuring a guy as a multi-breasted giant centipede, a bearded Nazi nun or a stockinged Peruvian Inca Orchid bitch.

"It's about bloody time you sprouted some testicles, mate," uttered Philippe.

"All in due time, my friend, all in due time."

"Are you going to take care of the lass right now?"

"That's the plan, Stan."

"Would you consider stopping first for a bite to eat, mate?"

"No can do," I said to the mouth. "We have to do this thing and head back to the Rehabilitation Center. I'll get you some fetus tacos as soon as that's done, deal?"

"I'll try not to perish."

A few minutes later I pulled up to Ampu-titties. I grabbed the weird little gun.

I handed the guy at the door a big bill and walked in, hoping I didn't looked as freaked-out on the outside as I felt.

I made a beeline for the cyber lounge and took a seat. When the usual guy came by to hand over the equipment, I handed him a twenty and told him I needed to see Marie to give her an important message.

"She's working, sir," he said.

"I know. I'm her boyfriend."

His eyes rolled up. Apparently he had heard that line before. Another twenty took care of his incredulousness and got me to the back room. I opened a small door that lead to the back room and walked into an area with white walls and bored-looking cyberwhores stuck inside private booths. They were all wearing headsets and in postures that looked more jaded than sexy. I could see their backs or sides. They were all working, which meant I could probably do my thing without being noticed.

Marie was easy to spot. Her elbows were propped up on a furry brown desk and she was chewing gum. Uncertainty filled my head and a cold feeling seized my guts. My feet refused to take another step in her direction.

"Don't fuck this up now, you bloody fool!" hissed Philippe.

"I... I can't do this," now that I was where I needed to be, the love I had once felt for her crept back into my heart and paralyzed me.

"Sure you fucking can, you gutless worm! Grow some cojones and do it now, you bloody cunt!"

Philippe's voice made a few women turn their heads, but none removed their headsets and I was sure they couldn't see me over the walls of their booths. I recalled Philippe's wet 9-inch tongue plopping onto my belly and red anger warmed my innards and unfroze my feet. Remembering that saliva-covered appendage sliding into Marie and the way her delicious, warm stump had flapped against my body like never before shot resolution into my brain with the undeniable power of rushing shame.

With a quick motion, I pulled the gun out and walked over to where Marie was sitting. I called to her. Philippe chuckled.

"David? Is that you?" asked Marie, removing her headset.

"Yeah, it's me."

"It's us, cunt!" screamed Philippe.

Marie stood up. Her mouth hung open. It made her look positively retarded. I brought the gun up shakily and clicked off the safety. Marie's face registered surprise, fear and anger. Her mouth moved as if she was about to say something. My finger wrapped around the trigger and squeezed.

A small needle buried itself below her left clavicle. She gasped and tensed. Instead of turning around and getting the hell out of there, I stood and watched Marie's face. Her skin bubbled and her body shook. Hair fell out as her scalp began to melt and her breasts slid drown her chest, pulling her top with them. Her eyeballs turned white and steamed in their sockets.

I turned for the door, glancing behind me. There was nothing but a big puddle of goo on the floor with small rivulets of smoke coming from it. The rest of the cyberwhores were still talking to losers over their headsets and only a few were scrunching up their noses at the smell coming from the puddle of melted flesh and bone.

Marie never screamed.

Philippe chuckled all the way to the car.

THIRTEEN

I calmly returned the gun to Tony.

"Did you go through with it?" he asked.

"I did, my friend." I hadn't processed it yet, so that was all I could say. However, Tony was not about to let it go at that.

"So, how do you feel now?"

"I... I don't know," I said. "A part of me is happy that she got what she deserved but..."

"Two parts of you are happy!" said Philippe.

"Listen, Gut, you need some time to let this sink in. You know, like twenty minutes or something. Then you need to get your life back on track and get your ass back to work."

"I know, it's just that now I'll never know why she did it," I said, realizing that maybe we could've had a future. "Maybe at some point she was going to come back on her hands and knees and beg me to take her back."

"You should've thought about that shit before you turned her into a pink puddle," said Tony.

I knew he was right. While Philippe was devouring fetus tacos, I got another text about a small man that was selling chicken, duck, alligator, snake, demon and ostrich baluts out of a cart near the park and hadn't paid MegaCorp anything in more than two months. Like an automaton, I went there, dragged the little Filipino man away from his cart kicking and screaming, dropped him in Tony's capable paws and headed home.

A sense of detachment had taken over me and I was in no mood to fight it. I went home, watched another Mellick V book and decided to wash away my crime with a long shower.

There was a knock at the door as I stepped out of the shower. I opened it wearing shorts and a smile. Two guys in silvery suits stood outside. One was about seven feet tall, sported a thick handlebar moustache and looked like he could knock someone out with a punch to the knee. The other was about two feet shorter, bald, and had one huge, droopy eye in the middle of his forehead.

The tiny Cyclops did the talking in a high-pitched voice. "Mr. Dedmon?"

"That's me," I said in a voice pregnant with confidence. "How may I help you, gentlemen?"

"We're here to talk to you about the unauthorized disposal of Marie Wilcox."

"It was him!" screamed Philippe in a shrill, desperate tone. "This bloody cunt has gone off his trolley! I told him not to do it!"

"You will have to excuse my friend, gentlemen, he's been under a lot of stress lately," I said. "I'll take care of it immediately... with the sharpest fucking knife I can find in this house!"

"No need for excuses or self-mutilation, sir," said the small man. "In any case, in the security footage we have from the Watchers installed in the back room of the Amputitties club your... friend there can clearly be heard egging you on and chuckling."

Fucking biomechanical eyes in the sky. For some unfathomable reason, it had never occurred to me to think that MegaCorp would have a surveillance system in one of its own clubs. Tony didn't think about it either. A mental lapse that would undoubtedly cost me my life. And possibly Tony's.

"Son of a bitch!" I said, punching myself in the thigh and feeling anger boiling in my chest. "If you have the footage, why the hell are you asking me about it?" I asked.

"It's standard procedure, Mr. Dedmon. Also, there are certain protocols followed whenever a MegaCorp employee is involved in an unauthorized disposal."

"I see. Should I get dressed and accompany you somewhere, gentlemen? Maybe to grab an endorphinated beer and see if we can work something out? After all, I only helped MegaCorp get rid of a nuisance, right?"

The small Cyclops nodded and then shook his head. I got the message: yes, you have to come with us; no, there will be no beer.

"Oh, mate, you've really fucked up big this time," said Philippe.

"Listen, you slimy, yellow, snaggletoothed parasite, I will finish you before they finish me, you got that?" I told Philippe through clenched teeth.

Apparently my voice carried with it enough spite to scare Philippe into silence.

After dressing unhurriedly and walking down with the two suited fellows to their waiting car, I was shoved into the backseat. The tall guy drove while the small one kept his droopy eye on me.

Ten minutes later I was inside a pink cell.

FOURTEEN

I woke up on my third day of imprisonment and fed Philippe some purple porridge. I got misty-eyed at the sight of the last acidophilus bacterium floating around lifeless in the toilet water. Then I decided to crap into my hand anyway and wait for the guard to come for the breakfast bowl. That small pleasure was keeping me sane and there was no reason to stop. As chance would have it, I never got to throw that last steaming turd at the pointy head of my molluscoid nemesis.

Midmorning had come and the walls were shaking more than usual. A commotion erupted at the end of the hallway and then the giant squid flew by the cell as if caught by an invisible net. I heard mad cackling and stomping feet. Tony arrived at my cell door—all smiles. The huge rat jingled some keys and in two seconds his muscular arms were opening the door that separated me from the outside world.

I was speechless for the first time in my life.

Tony was not. "Get a move on, you fool!"

I ran to the rat and wrapped my arms halfway around his thick chest.

Tony patted me on the back. "We can have this moment later, Gut, now we have to haul ass outta here before that stinky fucker wakes up and gets some more guards in here."

I nodded and signaled for him to lead the way.

As we ran down the hallway, we heard hissed commands. We hit the end of the hallway and turned the corner to the big processing room. The first sounds of violence reached my ears. A shot went off and my heart stopped. Then I saw what was going on.

Screw had something that resembled a medieval flail in both hands and was swinging it around and knocking squid guards down left and right. Gage was pumping a sawed-off shotgun with his nipple-covered arm. Star held monstrous axes on both hands. Her perfect figure moved around with the grace of a ballerina. Her red tresses spun around and mixed with the brown liquid that spurted from the decapitated guards that fell all around her like snake-tree scale-leaves on a windy day.

The surreal beauty of the scene stopped me in my tracks. Tony pushed past me and jumped into the middle of the action. The rat lifted a guard with his powerful rodent arms and slammed him down with such brute force that its gelatinous body exploded against the floor. A slimy chunk of guard smacked against my cheek and snapped me out of my daze.

I ran up to the first guard I saw and started pounding the shit of his foul, oppressive ass. His flesh felt like hard rubber but it broke under the hardest punches. The guard went down. I kicked his head in. A guttural, primal scream erupted from my throat and I looked for more guards.

Not long after, we stood victorious among a sea of dead and squirming tentacles. The stench was unbearable and we left without a word.

Outside, Gage hopped on the Amanda-bike, Star climbed on her Fugu fish and Screw, Tony and me climbed on Screw's most prized possession: a super-antique 1955 Cadillac El Dorado. With the grey, looming MegaCorp prison behind us and the orange sun sinking into the horizon in front, the most beautiful and victorious group of system-fuckers in recent history rode off hooting and hollering.

"You guys are fucking awesome," I said. "I guess this means we're starting a revolution!"

"Are you out of your mind?" asked Tony.

"No, but now that I know you're all pissed off at the system and willing to crush some heads, I thought we could..."

"Yeah, the system is a piece of shit, but we didn't get you out of there to start a revolution," said Tony. "Hell, if I had a death wish, I'd slap Bella's ass on one of her bad days."

"Then why did you get me out? Why did we kill all those

guards? What about being on camera? You know that your siege had to be seen. You're outlaws now!"

"Gut, you've seen the things we do to people who try to grow their own vegetables or forget to pay their bills," said Tony. "What do you think they'd do to you for killing a consumer? As soon as they started dipping your balls in flesh-eating bacteria and pumping rabid maggots into your colon, you'd tell them how you got the puddle-maker. When you gave them my name, they'd come for me. You know what I'd end up confessing? Some of the times I've let Screw and Gage off the hook. You see what I'm trying to tell you here, buddy? If you went down, we'd all go down with you. And as far as anyone seeing our liberating you goes, do you think we're that stupid?"

"I see..." was all I could say. Despite Tony's explanation, I knew they loved me and that their friendship was what really drove them to risk life and limb to get me out.

FIFTEEN

Gage managed to add four extra inches to my height and looking in the mirror is still a tad confusing for me. My new bald scalp and blue eyes still throw me off every morning. It will definitely take some time to get used to my new looks.

I now have Amanda's stomach and Gage and Screw were able to fully remove Philippe. I have a smaller stomach and a little scar where the mouth used to be.

I think about Philippe a lot. The British bastard comes to me in horrible nightmares in which he has become a giant mouth with no body. He screams at me for killing him and then chews me up.

Star and I have started dating and she sometimes cuts off her leg right before we make love. The feeling of her bloody stump against my skin is both pleasurable and scary. I'm is still trying to figure out exactly how I feel when she does that, but she loves fucking while we're are both high on Algolagnix and stabbing each other with ice picks, so I mostly just enjoy the moment and go with the flow. Dancing a little tango at the edge of death has certainly turned me into a much more mellow cat.

According to Tony, he only put the whole rescue mission together because he wanted to avoid the investigation that would arise if enough people saw the footage of me shooting what he calls the puddle-maker. As it stands right now, MegaCorp is half-heartedly looking for the old me and nobody else. A guy that owed Tony a few favors managed to put a virus inside the prison that gave all the Watchers cataracts and they shut down before the squid massacre. They're probably wondering how I managed to take care of two dozen guards all by myself and disappear. Let them wonder.

The plan now is for me to learn how to do skin grafts and penis splits from Star and join Screw's crew as the new me. I'm still deciding on a different name. I want it to be cool and dangerous sounding.

And revolution? Well, you need an army for that. Where better to recruit than the poor souls who come to mutilate themselves in order to feel something? I don't know, we'll see what the future brings, right?

Gabino Iglesias was born somewhere, but then he moved to a different place. He has worked as dog whisperer, witty communications professor, and ballerina assassin. Now he hides near a dumpster in Austin, Texas, where he works as a freelance journalist and impersonates a PhD student. His nonfiction has appeared in rags like *The New York Times, El Nuevo Día* and *Z Magazine*. The stuff that's made up has been published in places like *Bizarro Central, Paragraph Line, Divergent Magazine* and a few horror and bizarro anthologies. When not writing or fighting ninja squirrels, he devours books and regurgitates reviews that are published in places like *HorrorTalk, The Magazine of Bizarro Fiction, Zouch Magazine, Chiaroscuro, Black Heart Magazine, Horrorphilia, Buzzy Mag, The Lovecraft eZine* and a few others. He's currently working on overcoming his crippling hippopotomonstrosesquipedaliophobia. This is his first book.

BIZARRO BOOKS

CATALOG   SPRING 2012

ERASERHEAD PRESS

Your major resource for the bizarro fiction genre:

WWW.BIZARROCENTRAL.COM

Introduce yourselves to the bizarro fiction genre and all of its authors with the Bizarro Starter Kit series. Each volume features short novels and short stories by ten of the leading bizarro authors, designed to give you a perfect sampling of the genre for only $10.

BB-0X1
"The Bizarro Starter Kit"
(Orange)
Featuring D. Harlan Wilson, Carlton Mellick III, Jeremy Robert Johnson, Kevin L Donihe, Gina Ranalli, Andre Duza, Vincent W. Sakowski, Steve Beard, John Edward Lawson, and Bruce Taylor. **236 pages $10**

BB-0X2
"The Bizarro Starter Kit"
(Blue)
Featuring Ray Fracalossy, Jeremy C. Shipp, Jordan Krall, Mykle Hansen, Andersen Prunty, Eckhard Gerdes, Bradley Sands, Steve Aylett, Christian TeBordo, and Tony Rauch. **244 pages $10**

BB-0X2
"The Bizarro Starter Kit"
(Purple)
Featuring Russell Edson, Athena Villaverde, David Agranoff, Matthew Revert, Andrew Goldfarb, Jeff Burk, Garrett Cook, Kris Saknussemm, Cody Goodfellow, and Cameron Pierce **264 pages $10**

BB-001"The Kafka Effekt" D. Harlan Wilson — A collection of forty-four irreal short stories loosely written in the vein of Franz Kafka, with more than a pinch of William S. Burroughs sprinkled on top. **211 pages $14**

BB-002 "Satan Burger" Carlton Mellick III — The cult novel that put Carlton Mellick III on the map ... Six punks get jobs at a fast food restaurant owned by the devil in a city violently overpopulated by surreal alien cultures. **236 pages $14**

BB-003 "Some Things Are Better Left Unplugged" Vincent Sakwoski — Join The Man and his Nemesis, the obese tabby, for a nightmare roller coaster ride into this postmodern fantasy. **152 pages $10**

BB-004 "Shall We Gather At the Garden?" Kevin L Donihe — Donihe's Debut novel. Midgets take over the world, The Church of Lionel Richie vs. The Church of the Byrds, plant porn and more! **244 pages $14**

BB-005 "Razor Wire Pubic Hair" Carlton Mellick III — A genderless humandildo is purchased by a razor dominatrix and brought into her nightmarish world of bizarre sex and mutilation. **176 pages $11**

BB-006 "Stranger on the Loose" D. Harlan Wilson — The fiction of Wilson's 2nd collection is planted in the soil of normalcy, but what grows out of that soil is a dark, witty, otherworldly jungle... **228 pages $14**

BB-007 "The Baby Jesus Butt Plug" Carlton Mellick III — Using clones of the Baby Jesus for anal sex will be the hip sex fetish of the future. **92 pages $10**

BB-008 "Fishyfleshed" Carlton Mellick III — The world of the past is an illogical flatland lacking in dimension and color, a sick-scape of crispy squid people wandering the desert for no apparent reason. **260 pages $14**

BB-009 "Dead Bitch Army" Andre Duza — Step into a world filled with racist teenagers, cannibals, 100 warped Uncle Sams, automobiles with razor-sharp teeth, living graffiti, and a pissed-off zombie bitch out for revenge. **344 pages $16**

BB-010 "The Menstruating Mall" Carlton Mellick III — "The Breakfast Club meets Chopping Mall as directed by David Lynch." - Brian Keene **212 pages $12**

BB-011 "Angel Dust Apocalypse" Jeremy Robert Johnson — Meth-heads, man-made monsters, and murderous Neo-Nazis. "Seriously amazing short stories..." - Chuck Palahniuk, author of Fight Club **184 pages $11**

BB-012 "Ocean of Lard" Kevin L Donihe / Carlton Mellick III — A parody of those old Choose Your Own Adventure kid's books about some very odd pirates sailing on a sea made of animal fat. **176 pages $12**

BB-015 "Foop!" Chris Genoa — Strange happenings are going on at Dactyl, Inc, the world's first and only time travel tourism company.
"A surreal pie in the face!" - Christopher Moore **300 pages $14**

BB-020 "Punk Land" Carlton Mellick III — In the punk version of Heaven, the anarchist utopia is threatened by corporate fascism and only Goblin, Mortician's sperm, and a blue-mohawked female assassin named Shark Girl can stop them. **284 pages $15**

BB-027 "Siren Promised" Jeremy Robert Johnson & Alan M Clark — Nominated for the Bram Stoker Award. A potent mix of bad drugs, bad dreams, brutal bad guys, and surreal/incredible art by Alan M. Clark. **190 pages $13**

BB-031"Sea of the Patchwork Cats" Carlton Mellick III — A quiet dreamlike tale set in the ashes of the human race. For Mellick enthusiasts who also adore The Twilight Zone. **112 pages $10**

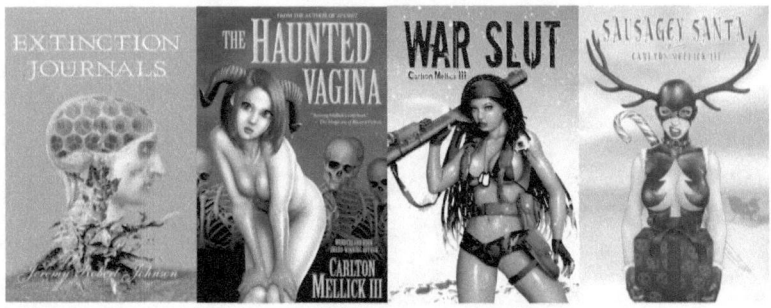

BB-032 **"Extinction Journals" Jeremy Robert Johnson** — An uncanny voyage across a newly nuclear America where one man must confront the problems associated with loneliness, insane dieties, radiation, love, and an ever-evolving cockroach suit with a mind of its own. **104 pages $10**

BB-037 **"The Haunted Vagina" Carlton Mellick III** — It's difficult to love a woman whose vagina is a gateway to the world of the dead. **132 pages $10**

BB-043 **"War Slut" Carlton Mellick III** — Part "1984," part "Waiting for Godot," and part action horror video game adaptation of John Carpenter's "The Thing." **116 pages $10**

BB-047 **"Sausagey Santa" Carlton Mellick III** — A bizarro Christmas tale featuring Santa as a piratey mutant with a body made of sausages. 124 pages $10

BB-048 **"Misadventures in a Thumbnail Universe" Vincent Sakowski** — Dive deep into the surreal and satirical realms of neo-classical Blender Fiction, filled with television shoes and flesh-filled skies. **120 pages $10**

BB-053 **"Ballad of a Slow Poisoner" Andrew Goldfarb** — Millford Mutterwurst sat down on a Tuesday to take his afternoon tea, and made the unpleasant discovery that his elbows were becoming flatter. **128 pages $10**

BB-055 **"Help! A Bear is Eating Me" Mykle Hansen** — The bizarro, heart-warming, magical tale of poor planning, hubris and severe blood loss... **150 pages $11**

BB-056 **"Piecemeal June" Jordan Krall** — A man falls in love with a living sex doll, but with love comes danger when her creator comes after her with crab-squid assassins. **90 pages $9**

BB-058 **"The Overwhelming Urge" Andersen Prunty** — A collection of bizarro tales by Andersen Prunty. **150 pages $11**

BB-059 **"Adolf in Wonderland" Carlton Mellick III** — A dreamlike adventure that takes a young descendant of Adolf Hitler's design and sends him down the rabbit hole into a world of imperfection and disorder. **180 pages $11**

BB-061 **"Ultra Fuckers" Carlton Mellick III** — Absurdist suburban horror about a couple who enter an upper middle class gated community but can't find their way out. **108 pages $9**

BB-062 **"House of Houses" Kevin L. Donihe** — An odd man wants to marry his house. Unfortunately, all of the houses in the world collapse at the same time in the Great House Holocaust. Now he must travel to House Heaven to find his departed fiancee. **172 pages $11**

BB-064 **"Squid Pulp Blues" Jordan Krall** — In these three bizarro-noir novellas, the reader is thrown into a world of murderers, drugs made from squid parts, deformed gun-toting veterans, and a mischievous apocalyptic donkey. **204 pages $12**

BB-065 **"Jack and Mr. Grin" Andersen Prunty** — "When Mr. Grin calls you can hear a smile in his voice. Not a warm and friendly smile, but the kind that seizes your spine in fear. You don't need to pay your phone bill to hear it. That smile is in every line of Prunty's prose." - Tom Bradley. **208 pages $12**

BB-066 **"Cybernetrix" Carlton Mellick III** — What would you do if your normal everyday world was slowly mutating into the video game world from Tron? **212 pages $12**

BB-072 **"Zerostrata" Andersen Prunty** — Hansel Nothing lives in a tree house, suffers from memory loss, has a very eccentric family, and falls in love with a woman who runs naked through the woods every night. **144 pages $11**

BB-073 "The Egg Man" Carlton Mellick III — It is a world where humans reproduce like insects. Children are the property of corporations, and having an enormous ten-foot brain implanted into your skull is a grotesque sexual fetish. Mellick's industrial urban dystopia is one of his darkest and grittiest to date. **184 pages $11**

BB-074 "Shark Hunting in Paradise Garden" Cameron Pierce — A group of strange humanoid religious fanatics travel back in time to the Garden of Eden to discover it is invested with hundreds of giant flying maneating sharks. **150 pages $10**

BB-075 "Apeshit" Carlton Mellick III - Friday the 13th meets Visitor Q. Six hipster teens go to a cabin in the woods inhabited by a deformed killer. An incredibly fucked-up parody of B-horror movies with a bizarro slant. **192 pages $12**

BB-076 "Fuckers of Everything on the Crazy Shitting Planet of the Vomit At smosphere" Mykle Hansen - Three bizarro satires. Monster Cocks, Journey to the Center of Agnes Cuddlebottom, and Crazy Shitting Planet. **228 pages $12**

BB-077 "The Kissing Bug" Daniel Scott Buck — In the tradition of Roald Dahl, Tim Burton, and Edward Gorey, comes this bizarro anti-war children's story about a bohemian conenose kissing bug who falls in love with a human woman. **116 pages $10**

BB-078 "MachoPoni" Lotus Rose — It's My Little Pony... *Bizarro* style! A long time ago Poniworld was split in two. On one side of the Jagged Line is the Pastel Kingdom, a magical land of music, parties, and positivity. On the other side of the Jagged Line is Dark Kingdom inhabited by an army of undead ponies. **148 pages $11**

BB-079 "The Faggiest Vampire" Carlton Mellick III — A Roald Dahl-esque children's story about two faggy vampires who partake in a mustache competition to find out which one is truly the faggiest. **104 pages $10**

BB-080 "Sky Tongues" Gina Ranalli — The autobiography of Sky Tongues, the biracial hermaphrodite actress with tongues for fingers. Follow her strange life story as she rises from freak to fame. **204 pages $12**

BB-081 **"Washer Mouth" Kevin L. Donihe** - A washing machine becomes human and pursues his dream of meeting his favorite soap opera star. **244 pages $11**

BB-082 **"Shatnerquake" Jeff Burk** - All of the characters ever played by William Shatner are suddenly sucked into our world. Their mission: hunt down and destroy the real William Shatner. **100 pages $10**

BB-083 **"The Cannibals of Candyland" Carlton Mellick III** - There exists a race of cannibals that are made of candy. They live in an underground world made out of candy. One man has dedicated his life to killing them all. **170 pages $11**

BB-084 **"Slub Glub in the Weird World of the Weeping Willows"** **Andrew Goldfarb** - The charming tale of a blue glob named Slub Glub who helps the weeping willows whose tears are flooding the earth. There are also hyenas, ghosts, and a voodoo priest **100 pages $10**

BB-085 **"Super Fetus" Adam Pepper** - Try to abort this fetus and he'll kick your ass! **104 pages $10**

BB-086 **"Fistful of Feet" Jordan Krall** - A bizarro tribute to spaghetti westerns, featuring Cthulhu-worshipping Indians, a woman with four feet, a crazed gunman who is obsessed with sucking on candy, Syphilis-ridden mutants, sexually transmitted tattoos, and a house devoted to the freakiest fetishes. **228 pages $12**

BB-087 **"Ass Goblins of Auschwitz" Cameron Pierce** - It's Monty Python meets Nazi exploitation in a surreal nightmare as can only be imagined by Bizarro author Cameron Pierce. **104 pages $10**

BB-088 **"Silent Weapons for Quiet Wars" Cody Goodfellow** - "This is high-end psychological surrealist horror meets bottom-feeding low-life crime in a techno-thrilling science fiction world full of Lovecraft and magic..." -John Skipp **212 pages $12**

BB-089 "Warrior Wolf Women of the Wasteland" Carlton Mellick III
— Road Warrior Werewolves versus McDonaldland Mutants...post-apocalyptic fiction has never been quite like this. **316 pages $13**

BB-091 "Super Giant Monster Time" Jeff Burk — A tribute to choose your own adventures and Godzilla movies. Will you escape the giant monsters that are rampaging the fuck out of your city and shit? Or will you join the mob of alien-controlled punk rockers causing chaos in the streets? What happens next depends on you. **188 pages $12**

BB-092 "Perfect Union" Cody Goodfellow — "Cronenberg's THE FLY on a grand scale: human/insect gene-spliced body horror, where the human hive politics are as shocking as the gore." -John Skipp. **272 pages $13**

BB-093 "Sunset with a Beard" Carlton Mellick III — 14 stories of surreal science fiction. **200 pages $12**

BB-094 "My Fake War" Andersen Prunty — The absurd tale of an unlikely soldier forced to fight a war that, quite possibly, does not exist. It's Rambo meets Waiting for Godot in this subversive satire of American values and the scope of the human imagination. **128 pages $11**

BB-095 "Lost in Cat Brain Land" Cameron Pierce — Sad stories from a surreal world. A fascist mustache, the ghost of Franz Kafka, a desert inside a dead cat. Primordial entities mourn the death of their child. The desperate serve tea to mysterious creatures. A hopeless romantic falls in love with a pterodactyl. And much more. **152 pages $11**

BB-096 "The Kobold Wizard's Dildo of Enlightenment +2" Carlton Mellick III — A Dungeons and Dragons parody about a group of people who learn they are only made up characters in an AD&D campaign and must find a way to resist their nerdy teenaged players and retarded dungeon master in order to survive. 232 **pages $12**

BB-098 "A Hundred Horrible Sorrows of Ogner Stump" Andrew Goldfarb — Goldfarb's acclaimed comic series. A magical and weird journey into the horrors of everyday life. **164 pages $11**

BB-099 "Pickled Apocalypse of Pancake Island" Cameron Pierce—A demented fairy tale about a pickle, a pancake, and the apocalypse. **102 pages $8**

BB-100 "Slag Attack" Andersen Prunty— Slag Attack features four visceral, noir stories about the living, crawling apocalypse.A slag is what survivors are calling the slug-like maggots raining from the sky, burrowing inside people, and hollowing out their flesh and their sanity. **148 pages $11**

BB-101 "Slaughterhouse High" Robert Devereaux—A place where schools are built with secret passageways, rebellious teens get zippers installed in their mouths and genitals, and once a year, on that special night, one couple is slaughtered and the bits of their bodies are kept as souvenirs. **304 pages $13**

BB-102 "The Emerald Burrito of Oz" John Skipp & Marc Levinthal —OZ IS REAL! Magic is real! The gate is really in Kansas! And America is finally allowing Earth tourists to visit this weird-ass, mysterious land. But when Gene of Los Angeles heads off for summer vacation in the Emerald City, little does he know that a war is brewing...a war that could destroy both worlds. **280 pages $13**

BB-103 "The Vegan Revolution... with Zombies" David Agranoff — When there's no more meat in hell, the vegans will walk the earth. **160 pages $11**

BB-104 "The Flappy Parts" Kevin L Donihe—Poems about bunnies, LSD, and police abuse. You know, things that matter. 132 **pages $11**

BB-105 "Sorry I Ruined Your Orgy" Bradley Sands—Bizarro humorist Bradley Sands returns with one of the strangest, most hilarious collections of the year. **130 pages $11**

BB-106 "Mr. Magic Realism" Bruce Taylor—Like Golden Age science fiction comics written by Freud, *Mr. Magic Realism* is a strange, insightful adventure that spans the furthest reaches of the galaxy, exploring the hidden caverns in the hearts and minds of men, women, aliens, and biomechanical cats. **152 pages $11**

BB-107 **"Zombies and Shit" Carlton Mellick III**—"Battle Royale" meets "Return of the Living Dead." Mellick's bizarro tribute to the zombie genre. **308 pages $13**

BB-108 **"The Cannibal's Guide to Ethical Living" Mykle Hansen**— Over a five star French meal of fine wine, organic vegetables and human flesh, a lunatic delivers a witty, chilling, disturbingly sane argument in favor of eating the rich.. **184 pages $11**

BB-109 **"Starfish Girl" Athena Villaverde**—In a post-apocalyptic underwater dome society, a girl with a starfish growing from her head and an assassin with sea anenome hair are on the run from a gang of mutant fish men. **160 pages $11**

BB-110 **"Lick Your Neighbor" Chris Genoa**—Mutant ninjas, a talking whale, kung fu masters, maniacal pilgrims, and an alcoholic clown populate Chris Genoa's surreal, darkly comical and unnerving reimagining of the first Thanksgiving. **303 pages $13**

BB-111 **"Night of the Assholes" Kevin L. Donihe**—A plague of assholes is infecting the countryside. Normal everyday people are transforming into jerks, snobs, dicks, and douchebags. And they all have only one purpose: to make your life a living hell.. **192 pages $11**

BB-112 **"Jimmy Plush, Teddy Bear Detective" Garrett Cook**—Hardboiled cases of a private detective trapped within a teddy bear body. **180 pages $11**

BB-113 **"The Deadheart Shelters" Forrest Armstrong**—The hip hop lovechild of William Burroughs and Dali... **144 pages $11**

BB-114 **"Eyeballs Growing All Over Me... Again" Tony Raugh**— Absurd, surreal, playful, dream-like, whimsical, and a lot of fun to read. **144 pages $11**

BB-115 **"Whargoul" Dave Brockie** — From the killing grounds of Stalingrad to the death camps of the holocaust. From torture chambers in Iraq to race riots in the United States, the Whargoul was there, killing and raping. **244 pages $12**

BB-116 **"By the Time We Leave Here, We'll Be Friends" J. David Osborne** — A David Lynchian nightmare set in a Russian gulag, where its prisoners, guards, traitors, soldiers, lovers, and demons fight for survival and their own rapidly deteriorating humanity. **168 pages $11**

BB-117 **"Christmas on Crack" edited by Carlton Mellick III** — Perverted Christmas Tales for the whole family! . . . as long as every member of your family is over the age of 18. **168 pages $11**

BB-118 **"Crab Town" Carlton Mellick III** — Radiation fetishists, balloon people, mutant crabs, sail-bike road warriors, and a love affair between a woman and an H-Bomb. This is one mean asshole of a city. Welcome to Crab Town. **100 pages $8**

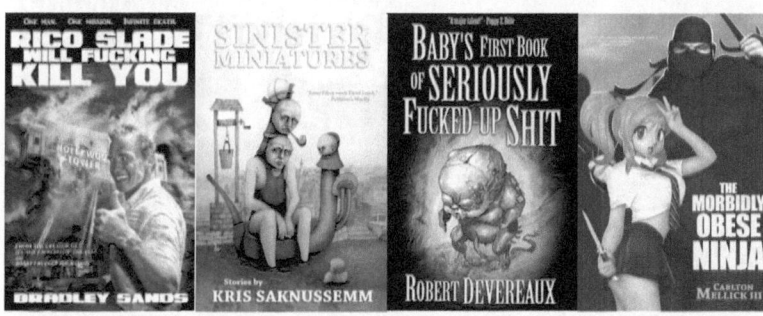

BB-119 **"Rico Slade Will Fucking Kill You" Bradley Sands** — Rico Slade is an action hero. Rico Slade can rip out a throat with his bare hands. Rico Slade's favorite food is the honey-roasted peanut. Rico Slade will fucking kill everyone. A novel. **122 pages $8**

BB-120 **"Sinister Miniatures" Kris Saknussemm** — The definitive collection of short fiction by Kris Saknussemm, confirming that he is one of the best, most daring writers of the weird to emerge in the twenty-first century. **180 pages $11**

BB-121 **"Baby's First Book of Seriously Fucked up Shit" Robert Devereaux** — Ten stories of the strange, the gross, and the just plain fucked up from one of the most original voices in horror. **176 pages $11**

BB-122 **"The Morbidly Obese Ninja" Carlton Mellick III** — These days, if you want to run a successful company . . . you're going to need a lot of ninjas. **92 pages $8**

BB-123 **"Abortion Arcade" Cameron Pierce** — An intoxicating blend of body horror and midnight movie madness, reminiscent of early David Lynch and the splatterpunks at their most sublime. **172 pages $11**

BB-124 **"Black Hole Blues" Patrick Wensink** — A hilarious double helix of country music and physics. **196 pages $11**

BB-125 **"Barbarian Beast Bitches of the Badlands" Carlton Mellick III** — Three prequels and sequels to *Warrior Wolf Women of the Wasteland*. **284 pages $13**

BB-126 **"The Traveling Dildo Salesman" Kevin L. Donihe** — A nightmare comedy about destiny, faith, and sex toys. Also featuring Donihe's most lurid and infamous short stories: *Milky Agitation, Two-Way Santa, The Helen Mower, Living Room Zombies,* and *Revenge of the Living Masturbation Rag.* **108 pages $8**

BB-127 **"Metamorphosis Blues" Bruce Taylor** — Enter a land of love beasts, intergalactic cowboys, and rock 'n roll. A land where Sears Catalogs are doorways to insanity and men keep mysterious black boxes. Welcome to the monstrous mind of Mr. Magic Realism. **136 pages $11**

BB-128 **"The Driver's Guide to Hitting Pedestrians" Andersen Prunty** — A pocket guide to the twenty-three most painful things in life, written by the most well-adjusted man in the universe. **108 pages $8**

BB-129 **"Island of the Super People" Kevin Shamel** — Four students and their anthropology professor journey to a remote island to study its indigenous population. But this is no ordinary native culture. They're super heroes and villains with flesh costumes and out-landish abilities like self-detonation, musical eyelashes, and microwave hands. **194 pages $11**

BB-130 **"Fantastic Orgy" Carlton Mellick III** — Shark Sex, mutant cats, and strange sexually transmitted diseases. Featuring the stories: *Candy-coated, Ear Cat, Fantastic Orgy, City Hobgoblins,* and *Porno in August.* **136 pages $9**

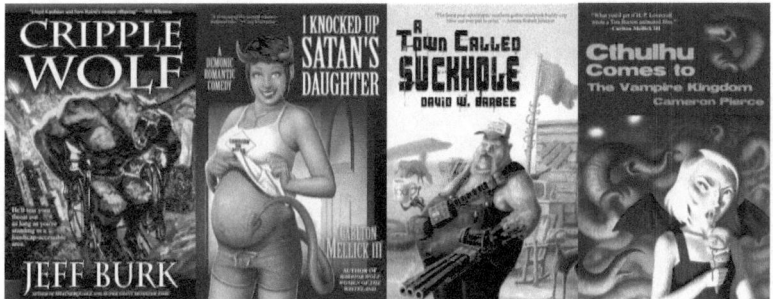

BB-131 **"Cripple Wolf" Jeff Burk** — Part man. Part wolf. 100% crippled. Also including *Punk Rock Nursing Home, Adrift with Space Badgers, Cook for Your Life, Just Another Day in the Park, Frosty and the Full Monty*, and *House of Cats*. **152 pages $10**

BB-132 **"I Knocked Up Satan's Daughter" Carlton Mellick III** — An adorable, violent, fantastical love story. A romantic comedy for the bizarro fiction reader. **152 pages $10**

BB-133 **"A Town Called Suckhole" David W. Barbee** — Far into the future, in the nuclear bowels of post-apocalyptic Dixie, there is a town. A town of derelict mobile homes, ancient junk, and mutant wildlife. A town of slack jawed rednecks who bask in the splendors of moonshine and mud boggin'. A town dedicated to the bloody and demented legacy of the Old South. A town called Suckhole. **144 pages $10**

BB-134 **"Cthulhu Comes to the Vampire Kingdom" Cameron Pierce** — What you'd get if H. P. Lovecraft wrote a Tim Burton animated film. **148 pages $11**

BB-135 **"I am Genghis Cum" Violet LeVoit** — From the savage Arctic tundra to post-partum mutations to your missing daughter's unmarked grave, join visionary madwoman Violet LeVoit in this non-stop eight-story onslaught of full-tilt Bizarro punk lit thrills. **124 pages $9**

BB-136 **"Haunt" Laura Lee Bahr** — A tripping-balls Los Angeles noir, where a mysterious dame drags you through a time-warping Bizarro hall of mirrors. **316 pages $13**

BB-137 **"Amazing Stories of the Flying Spaghetti Monster" edited by Cameron Pierce** — Like an all-spaghetti evening of Adult Swim, the Flying Spaghetti Monster will show you the many realms of His Noodly Appendage. Learn of those who worship him and the lives he touches in distant, mysterious ways. **228 pages $12**

BB-138 **"Wave of Mutilation" Douglas Lain** — A dream-pop exploration of modern architecture and the American identity, *Wave of Mutilation* is a Zen finger trap for the 21st century. **100 pages $8**

BB-139 **"Hooray for Death!" Mykle Hansen** — Famous Author Mykle Hansen draws unconventional humor from deaths tiny and large, and invites you to laugh while you can. **128 pages $10**

BB-140 **"Hypno-hog's Moonshine Monster Jamboree" Andrew Goldfarb** — Hicks, Hogs, Horror! Goldfarb is back with another strange illustrated tale of backwoods weirdness. **120 pages $9**

BB-141 **"Broken Piano For President" Patrick Wensink** — A comic masterpiece about the fast food industry, booze, and the necessity to choose happiness over work and security. **372 pages $15**

BB-142 **"Please Do Not Shoot Me in the Face" Bradley Sands** — A novel in three parts, *Please Do Not Shoot Me in the Face: A Novel*, is the story of one boy detective, the worst ninja in the world, and the great American fast food wars. It is a novel of loss, destruction, and--incredibly--genuine hope. **224 pages $12**

BB-143 **"Santa Steps Out" Robert Devereaux** — Sex, Death, and Santa Claus ... The ultimate erotic Christmas story is back. **294 pages $13**

BB-144 **"Santa Conquers the Homophobes" Robert Devereaux** — "I wish I could hope to ever attain one-thousandth the perversity of Robert Devereaux's toenail clippings." - Poppy Z. Brite **316 pages $13**

BB-145 **"We Live Inside You" Jeremy Robert Johnson** — "Jeremy Robert Johnson is dancing to a way different drummer. He loves language, he loves the edge, and he loves us people. These stories have range and style and wit. This is entertainment... and literature."- Jack Ketchum **188 pages $11**

BB-146 **"Clockwork Girl" Athena Villaverde** — Urban fairy tales for the weird girl in all of us. Like a combination of Francesca Lia Block, Charles de Lint, Kathe Koja, Tim Burton, and Hayao Miyazaki, her stories are cute, kinky, edgy, magical, provocative, and strange, full of poetic imagery and vicious sexuality. **160 pages $10**

BB-147 **"Armadillo Fists" Carlton Mellick III** — A weird-as-hell gangster story set in a world where people drive giant mechanical dinosaurs instead of cars. **168 pages $11**

BB-148 **"Gargoyle Girls of Spider Island" Cameron Pierce** — Four college seniors venture out into open waters for the tropical party weekend of a lifetime. Instead of a teenage sex fantasy, they find themselves in a nightmare of pirates, sharks, and sex-crazed monsters. **100 pages $8**

BB-149 **"The Handsome Squirm" by Carlton Mellick III** — Like Franz Kafka's *The Trial* meets an erotic body horror version of *The Blob*. **158 pages $11**

BB-150 **"Tentacle Death Trip" Jordan Krall** — It's *Death Race 2000* meets H. P. Lovecraft in bizarro author Jordan Krall's best and most suspenseful work to date. **224 pages $12**

BB-151 **"The Obese" Nick Antosca** — Like Alfred Hitchcock's *The Birds*... but with obese people. **108 pages $10**

BB-152 **"All-Monster Action!" Cody Goodfellow** — The world gave him a blank check and a demand: Create giant monsters to fight our wars. But Dr. Otaku was not satisfied with mere chaos and mass destruction.... **216 pages $12**

BB-153 **"Ugly Heaven" Carlton Mellick III** — Heaven is no longer a paradise. It was once a blissful utopia full of wonders far beyond human comprehension. But the afterlife is now in ruins. It has become an ugly, lonely wasteland populated by strange monstrous beasts, masturbating angels, and sad man-like beings wallowing in the remains of the once-great Kingdom of God. **106 pages $8**

BB-154 **"Space Walrus" Kevin L. Donihe** — Walter is supposed to go where no walrus has ever gone before, but all this astronaut walrus really wants is to take it easy on the intense training, escape the chimpanzee bullies, and win the love of his human trainer Dr. Stephanie. **160 pages $11**

www.ingramcontent.com/pod-product-compliance
Lightning Source LLC
Chambersburg PA
CBHW020729250626
47155CB00006B/2225